ARKED

TRIBES, #6

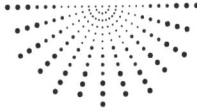

MILANA JACKS

PROLOGUE

TRIBES SERIES QUICK REFERENCE

*T*ribes series takes place on a planet called Nomra Prime. Thus far, we have the Ka and the Ra tribe that signed a peace treaty after eons of wars. On both sides, females and young are almost nonexistent, and the Ka males are near extinction.

Their alien classification is *Predator*. They're dual-form aliens. Their hunting form is a hunter and often stands as tall as a horse with exposed large sharp teeth, meaning the hunter's lips don't cover the teeth. They have large erect ears, which make them appear bigger and more frightening. They're extremely fit and agile, and can execute leaps we (humans) consider impossible.

Most tribes can be united under a single "King" they designate by adding -i to the tribe name. So for Ka tribe, it's Kai where -i at the end indicates a male who is a leader of the Ka tribe, the top of their food chain and this male always eats first.

Inside a single tribe, an earl governs a smaller territory called an earldom. There can be many many earldoms in any one tribe.

Portal: a spatial shortcut to another place on the planet. A closed portal, meaning a vertical golden line, is not visible to the human eye.

Main Characters:

Hart : Ka tribal leader, Alpha of the Ka tribe. His designation is Kai.

Stephanie: Hart's human. Believed to be Amti.

Nar: Hart's brother and second strongest of the Ka males.

Michelle: Nar's human. Believed to be Aoa.

Mas: Ka tribe portal genius.

Tatyana: Mas' human. Believed to be Eme.

Tis: Mas's brother.

Ark: Ra tribe's Alpha, meaning the strongest of the Ra males but not an elected leader, meaning the Ra do not have a single "King" named Rai where -i at the end indicates his "kingship" over other tribal members. Hart's frenemy.

Sha-male: a male who performs religious rites, sacrifices, prayers (priest, imam, etc)

Gur: Earl in the Ra tribe. Wants war.

Feli: Second to Gur in Gur's earldom.

Nen: Largest and most feared predator. Om tribal leader, Alpha of the Om tribe. His designation is Omi.

Tash: Ark's older brother. Earl.

Imani: Tash's human. Believed to be Bera.

Dani: Ark and Tash's mother

Lena: Believed to be Mae.

The Lore: Tribes worship the female. Goddesses are admired, feared, and respected. They're believed to be returning as human females so that they may walk the lands again.

2

Bera: Goddess of fertility and war. Most worshiped.

Aimea: Goddess of doom. Most feared.

Herea: Goddess of hunt and harmony. Most popular.

Amti: Goddess of madness and lust.

Aoa: Goddess of thunder and pain. Patron goddess of the Ka tribe.

Eme: Goddess of blood and grace. Also called the Bloodletter. Herea's daughter.

Mae: Goddess of fire and lies. Aoa's mother. Patron goddess of the Ra tribe.

Ila: Goddess of wind and desire.

Locations:

Kalia: Ka tribe capital. Near the Ra border. Suffered extensive structural damage during the wars.

Blood Dunes: Ancient grounds haunted by Eme, the Bloodletter. Currently, Ra territory under governance of earl Tash.

Mount Omila: Om territory. Birds of Prey live here.

Ralna: Ra tribe capital.

CHAPTER ONE

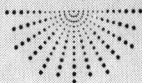

ARK

*W*hen fighting a war on enemy territory, one should survey the terrain, take stock of enemy positions, and count their numbers. Then one should strategize the conquest. Since I'm alone in enemy territory, I have accepted that I'm suicidal. In the spirit of my mission—which is highly unlikely to succeed—I've identified a single target that, if hit at the center, will make the mission a success. That target is a human female I've quietly kept in the back of my mind ever since I met her.

My focus on her didn't start out as deliberate as it is now.

No, over time, her image simmered in the back of my mind, taunting me with promises of fiery nights spent making pups. I wondered why this female had invaded my thoughts, and since I couldn't come up with a reason, I ignored her, thinking she'd go away.

But then, the goddesses showed me the way. The way led to Ralna's market, the most dangerous place I could possibly hang out in the night before the games.

If I'm spotted, my mother will send assassins after me.

If I'm spotted, my brother might kill me.

If I'm spotted, their allies might kill me.

And yet I've been coming here for many spans, hunting my target and identifying her movement patterns, likes, and dislikes so that I can win her in the games.

Luckily for me, my little stepbrother, Vor, is predictable in how he goes about his span, and since he's wooing Mae, goddess of fire and lies, her patterns have become predictable as well.

Around midspan, Vor takes Mae for a stroll through Ralna. He does this nearly every span, and since I've stalked the pair for over a cycle now, I no longer need to swim under their raft in the river beneath the palace, but simply wait behind Jal's stand for their arrival.

The sunrays hitting the right side of my face tell me it's time that the couple would reach the raft dock. It's only a matter of moments before they walk into the streets of Ralna, which are designed as the market space, Mae's favorite place on Nomra Prime.

That's her declaration, not mine. There are nicer places in this land than the crowded, stinky market that sells things I don't need.

Like our Ka neighbors, the Ra used to be self-sustaining and rustic, but space exploration has changed how we conduct business now. Other aliens trade, and we adopted some of what we uncovered in our travels. A mistake, in my opinion, but the market is popular with my tribe, so I'll keep it when I'm their Rai.

Stepping back into the shadows, gaze focused on the corner she'll round when coming from the raft dock, I wait.

My hunter senses her before I see her, and I purr low in my chest, licking the tips of my pointy canines, her scent inviting me for a meal. She walks around the bend wearing the combination of human and Ra female fashions that's setting the latest trend among the few females we have left in our tribe.

I'm happy nobody saw her a few spans ago in those impractical blue pants most humans we found wore. Those things cover most of her legs, and I prefer to see her legs. They're pleasing to my eyes.

This span, she wears a minidress made of thick forest-green fabric and thigh-high black leather boots. On top, she's covered under Vor's fur, which he purchased rather than killed and made for himself.

I pat my Ka hunter fur that hangs around my shoulders, the one I killed and made for myself, and bring it closer around my neck just as a sharp winter wind tears through the city.

Mae rubs her hands together and blows into them.

Vor offers her his gloves.

The male must like her. He's not exactly known for charity or for courting females. Then again, no other female is as pretty as this one. The human the goddess of fire has inhabited has long, wavy, fire-red hair and large green eyes framed in long dark lashes. There are brown spots on her nose that make her appear even younger than a barely adult female, and when she smiles, her eyes crease at the corners and lift.

When she frowns, her supple mouth also creases at the corners.

Looking at her from afar always makes me smile. That's because when I'm around, she looks different. Mainly, her pale face turns bright red when she's angry, and I make her angry often.

Vor tucks her hand under his elbow while Mae's gaze sweeps the crowd until it reaches Jal's stand. I dip my gaze and wait till the couple walk past me. Under the cover of my hood, I step onto the street and follow them as they walk through the market.

My tribemates whisper about them, and I listen in for the latest rumors.

The games will open at dawn, and my people believe Vor will win, but what they don't know is that I intend to compete. I gifted Mae with coins and jewels, and although she believes I did it out of charity, I did not.

Everything has a price, and I bought a favor with a goddess. Now, I just have to remind her that she owes me one.

Abruptly, the couple stop in the middle of the street. I pivot and pick up a pair of furry white gloves. They're half the size of my palm, and while keeping an eye on Mae and Vor, who seem to be lost in each other's whispers, their smiles and other pleasantries nauseating me, I ask the merchant, "How much for the gloves?"

"More than you can afford. Get out of here."

Now, most males reserve their hunting nature for hunting on four legs. I don't. I'm always one and the same, my eyes more often the silver of my hunter form than the white of a male. Therefore, now I would really enjoy ripping out the merchant's throat.

Keeping that happy thought at the forefront of my mind, I smile and flick a coin at his chest before pocketing the gloves. I turn toward the couple just as Vor's face nears Mae's, their lips almost touching.

Fuck no.

I sprint through the crowd, knocking over a ceramic statue of my mother. The people shout as the merchandise breaks on the stone, jagged pieces bouncing and cutting people. Vor lifts his head and starts issuing orders, attempting to calm the chaos.

I use the opportunity to sneak up behind Mae. Spinning

her by the shoulders, I kiss her on the lips, then check on Vor. He's walking away, shouting at the male he believes caused the ruckus.

Mae is riveted to the ground, her eyes wide and lips parted.

"Ark," she whispers. "What are you doing here?"

"Came for the games. You missed me?"

Her cheeks turn pink. "Ha! I picked my male already."

I smile. "I know. The games are just a formality."

"I don't mean you," she hisses.

"Mae." Vor waves her over as he speaks with a male I don't recognize, and the human gives me a victorious look before walking away with her nose turned up. I smirk while she sashays to Vor, who immediately scents me on her. I raise my hood so he doesn't spot my location.

There will be plenty of time to kill my little brother, but so little time to win the female who embodies the goddess of fire and lies.

Three spans, two nights, one winner. The games start at dawn.

CHAPTER TWO

LENA

The last four years of my life on Earth, I lived in San Diego, California, so I haven't seen snow this up close and personal since I was about four. Or was it six? Hard to keep track when you've traveled as often as I have.

Well, not exactly.

I call hopping from foster home to foster home traveling, but beyond that, I am, in fact, well traveled. Domestic USA at least, and now even across the stars all the way to Nomra Prime.

For an eighteen-year-old with no parents or prospects, buying her heart's desire at Ralna's marketplace thousands of light years away from Earth is exciting. Maybe a bit too exciting when Nomra Prime's most infuriating male decides to kiss me while I'm out and about with his brother who wants to kill him.

Wrapped in the finest fabrics Ralna has to offer, my hair done by predator females who can braid Viking style in under a half hour, I try slipping out of the grip Vor has on my arm.

"Who was that?" he asks.

"I don't know," I lie, and I love lying. Every time I lie, I get a jolt of pleasant, happy energy.

Vor's claws are digging into my skin, and I yelp when he tightens his hold.

Vor hates Ark more than anything in the world. He's told me so, and I don't blame him. Ark is easy to hate. He's arrogant, imposing, and controlling, and everything seems to come easily to him, even the hard things, like, you know, trying to kill his big brother Tash.

Most times, Vor and I hate on Ark together.

Even more times, I lie about hating him.

Vor sniffs my cheek. "He's risking his life showing up here. Why?"

I shake off his hold. "Ask him."

Vor narrows his eyes. "I thought you hated him."

"I do."

His beard scrapes my cheek as he bends and whispers at my ear. "I scent him on your mouth."

An angry Vor is a dangerous animal, one nobody in the palace wants to push over the edge, myself included, and while everyone tells me I'm Mae, goddess of fire and lies, the patron goddess of the Ra tribe, I'm also five foot eight and one hundred fortyish pounds, with blunt teeth and blunt painted fingernails, compared to Vor's six-seven, two hundred plus pounds and sharp teeth and claws.

He can eat me for breakfast quite literally, so when he seethes and sneers around my throat, I pet his beast.

Stepping back, I look up, but not into his eyes so that he's not feeling challenged. I stare at his perfectly straight nose and chiseled cheekbones. Vor is a handsome male. He really is. Smiling kindly while my heart races, I reach out and stroke his cheek. "Your people are watching," I remind him. "You can't show them weakness. Jealousy can be interpreted as an insecurity, and that's a weakness." I rise on my toes, and he meets me halfway for a soft peck on the lips.

"There," I say, "your scent on my lips." Swallowing, I finally look up and lock eyes with his silver ones. They blaze with lust and the promise of endurance in bed for my first time when I lose my virginity tomorrow night.

"My scent is the first and last scent on your lips. Always, Mae."

"Always, Vor," I lie.

Vor's not my first. Back in high school, Brian Longcorn kissed me in the shed. We were dirty from fixing our bicycles and smeared grease all over each other's bodies as we made out. We were fifteen, and of the pair of us, I made it to sixteen. He didn't.

One year on Veterans Day, he stayed up late with his cousins from out of town, and he drank, did drugs, and drowned in the lake. I had no idea he couldn't swim.

Vor pulls my hand, jerking me out of my thoughts. As if nothing happened, he rests my palm over his elbow, and we continue strolling through the marketplace.

The tribemates sneak glances our way, looking a little worried, but that's nothing out of the ordinary. They fear him. As they should. Vor kills at the drop of a hat, thereby ruling the people from a place of fear, not respect or compassion.

We enter the center of the market, and since the royals are holding the games tomorrow, it's more crowded than usual. People are bumping into us, and soon enough, we're stopped while his guards scream at the people to make room for us to stroll through.

But the people also want to see.

They're whispering, chanting Mae's name.

Vor's growl becomes a permanent sound hovering above me like a threat while I'm trying to smile and greet the people shuffling to make way for their royalty—Vor is technically their prince born of two ruling parents—but it's really hard to clear the path for the prince when he's strolling with someone they believe is their goddess.

They want to be closer to what they consider divine.

I can see it in their eyes.

The pull is too great, and I'm getting anxious that a fight will break out if any male approaches me.

"Vor," I say.

His jaw is set tight, so tight he might just crush his teeth.

"Vor," I repeat a little louder and squeeze his arm.

"They're whispering," he says through gritted teeth.

"What about?"

"Him."

Ark. The Ra prince can't say his name. I can, though. I say it before I sleep when I stroke myself. Nobody has to know that, least of all Ark. Or Vor, for that matter. Yeah, better keep that shit to myself.

"What are the rumors?" His mother will ask, and I want to know as well. Rumors people spread matter.

"They're saying Ark is here to claim Mae."

"Duh."

Vor glares.

I cough. "Du-h. Got something stuck in my throat. Anyway, go on. What else?" I tug at him, trying to get him to walk back, but we're pretty much trapped within the crowd.

"There's no space for all the people who want to be here," I say. "We shouldn't have come today. Let's go back." The square isn't big enough for the crowd. We ought to expand the marketplace.

Vor places a hand on my throat, the hunter animal showing me his silver eyes, threatening me. "Are you afraid of a few peasants, Goddess?"

"I am not," I lie.

"I can protect you."

Oh, I know that. In his mind, he doesn't need to expand the marketplace. Instead, he'll order half the market's people slaughtered so he can have a nice stroll whenever he feels like it. "I don't need protection, predator," I say in the way I've heard Imani speak as Bera.

Vor can't tell when I lie. I don't think anyone can, and so I do it. And I lie because it works and has kept me alive all this time at the palace.

Vor loosens his hold and strokes my pulse. "Then why do you want to leave?"

"Let the people whisper whatever they like. It's what people do. And let us leave them to their whispers. The turnout for the games tomorrow will be historic because of Ark's appearance now, and since you will win the games, the Sha will write about you for centuries to come. Let the people whisper."

He kisses me, his lips warm and inviting, his scent fresh and citrusy. "When did you become so wise?"

When I realized your mother is a conniving bitch who wants to chop my head off. "When I met your mother. I'm learning from her." The mention of his mother reminds Vor of how to behave in public. According to her, he can't show his anger, or any emotions, for that matter. She believes people who show how they feel are easily manipulated, and she'd hate for anyone to manipulate her son. She likes to be the only one who does that.

Vor nods in agreement, and we turn, making our way back to the palace.

"You will make a fine Raiyes," he says.

That's what I'm afraid off. I need to go back to playing dumb the way I often do. Makes people not think about me as much. His mother needs to not think about me. If she smells brains in addition to my youth and good looks, she'll

14

kill me. Maybe she'll kill me anyway as soon as I deliver Vor a baby, but I have a better chance of surviving the palace court if I play stupid and live in a lie. She believes I'm head over heels for her son.

She's not wrong.

But I lie about which son.

CHAPTER THREE

LENA

*V*or enjoys nightly gatherings. I think it gives him an excuse to drink and get stoned on the smoke from the fire. The priests, called the Sha, light bonfires and throw herbs on the flames that create smoke with different scents that make people light-headed.

On Earth, we call it stoned.

These guys would love pot. Hell, I love pot. Loved. No pot here, but plenty of other herbs that make me smile all night long.

Which is a blessing, I'd say.

Because every night I sit with Dani, who is Vor's mother and the current Raiyes of the Ra tribe. If she wasn't a gray-furred huntress, I'd think she could shape-shift into a cobra. Sometimes, when I'm a bit stoned (like I am now), I gaze up at Dani from my bed of fur laid out on the steps right under her throne and picture a cobra sitting in her place.

And this evening, Dani wears a deep green outfit, so a cobra is a good fit. She sits with one leg crossed over the other, leather ierto falling over one slender thigh. On top, she wears a black leather corset with silver bra cups. A silver mesh belt hugs her belly.

Dani's hair is gray, almost platinum like Ark's, and the way she sits, all regal, beautiful, and important, she makes everyone feel watched and controlled.

This is her resting-bitch position.

The thought of her resting-bitch position makes me snort my drink, some sort of brew between wine and beer. It used to taste gross to me because it has the consistency of vegetable oil, but I got used to it.

I got used to lots of things.

I had to, or I would have died of depression and hopelessness along with Theodora in the ship. Imani helped me and my sister carry on and even to think of our crashed-on-a-predators-planet misfortune as good fortune. I count the good fortunes, our blessings daily, lest I forget my God in the midst of the goddesses.

Imani, a woman who couldn't get pregnant on Earth, is now gonna have twins with an awesome hot older dude who thinks she's a goddess.

My sister found her one true love in a male who treats her like she's a goddess.

Tomorrow, every one of these males will compete for the right to breed me. Vor will win, albeit not by might or sword, but by clever manipulation, mostly done by his mother. That's not to say Vor is a helpless little mama's boy. He is plenty conniving on his own.

It annoys me he won't compete in earnest. He ought to. The games are designed to test a male's fitness. The fittest wins, and I've been looking forward to the fitness games since I heard about them. What can I say? I also love football.

Standing, I lift my cup. "May the favored predator win."

Some males lift their cups, but most stare past me. I realize I should've said fittest, but I'm too stoned to care

17

about Dani and what she'll think of my little outburst. I should probably go to bed. Yawning, I cover my mouth with the back of my hand and have turned to leave when I run into Dani.

She smiles, a tilt of her mouth. "A Raiyes must learn to hold her exuberant joy and liquor, as well as prayer smoke."

"I'm not a Raiyes," I say.

She hums, liking that.

"I'm never gonna be a great Raiyes like you. I am prey, and prey is weak under the influence. But I'm lucky to always have you."

Dani's eyes crinkle at the corners. "Awww, my sweet pet." She pats my head. "It's a big span tomorrow for you and us all. Vor will escort you." She pauses, watching me, expecting something from me. What, though, I have no idea.

"Okay," I say, the same way I said okay to one of my foster mothers when she asked me to lie when Ms. Lane, my PE teacher, asked about belt marks across my back.

"Vor!" Dani shrieks, almost making my ears bleed. With a wave of her hand, Vor materializes next to her, defiance in his gaze. He dislikes it when she displays such power over him in public. He's not her bitch boy, but she likes to keep him in line and remind him who's really running the Ra tribe, and she does that in subtle ways so that the tribe doesn't notice but Vor does.

She doesn't snap her fingers when she calls for him, but that's what this looks like and Vor knows it. Once he arrives and we set off, Dani returns to her throne in a flutter of ierto pieces cut at the hems and carefully designed with opulence in mind. The way she grips the throne as she sits down shows she's displeased about something, and since her last conversation was with me, she must be displeased with me. Maybe *okay* doesn't work with her as it did with my foster mom.

Ms. Lane at school didn't buy the belt marks story I fed her (I wasn't such a great liar back then), but she did nothing about her instinct. All my teachers, bar one, never went that extra mile for me. They should've. That's what adults should do. That's what people in power should do. Take care that their people are cared for. Well, at least by my definition. Not Dani's, that's for sure.

Dani is a predator. As is Vor, who now leads me by the hand through a maze of hallways until we reach my rooms, or rather Mae's birthplace, the same place Tash brought me to. Dani has tried to move me out of the room, but I begged her to let me stay. It didn't work until Vor stepped in and basically told her I am to be housed in any room in the palace I wished. That declaration started Dani's and my rocky relationship.

Secretly, she hates me for many things, and one of them is taking away her precious boy. I guess that's normal. Maybe all moms are that way with their sons. Or daughters. I wouldn't know. Never met my mom.

At the massive doors that lead to my rooms, careful with his sharp claws, Vor lifts my chin. "Are you well, Lena?"

I like it when he says my name. I smile. "I'm thinking about tomorrow's games," I lie.

"Nervous?" He kisses me, and I return the kiss with my tongue. We make out, and since my eyes are open, in the corner of my right eye I see the shadows at the end of the hallway move. The torches dim, flames barely a flicker of light. Heat that feels like lava inside me rushes up my body and burns on my face.

I gasp, shocked at my body's response to Vor. Do I have the hots for him? Does Mae?

Vor steps back, a claw over his scorched mouth, a frown on his face. His white eyes search mine for an answer, and I better give him one, because I think I burned him. "Let's save the best for tomorrow night," I say. I'll pick him, and then he'll spend the night with me. It's a done deal.

Vor chuckles. "As you wish, Lena."

"I like that you use my real name instead of her name."

"Mae's?"

I nod.

He licks his lips, pretending the swelling sore he got from the burn doesn't exist. Yup, his goddess Mae, whose spirit resides inside me, lit up my body, and I burned his lips. *What the fuckery, Mae?* I say in my head, hoping the goddess will speak with me the same way Bera speaks with Imani.

"Sleep well," Vor says.

"You too."

Like a gentleman, he picks up my hand and kisses the top of it, then curtsies the way I told him royals did on Earth. With a smile, I enter my room.

A callused palm slaps over my mouth.

A hard body presses mine against the door.

Silver eyes blaze, Ark's hunter is agitated, threatening my life.

His ears twitch as he likely listens for Vor's retreating footsteps.

I knee him in the balls.

Ark grunts, bends slightly, then shows me his sharp teeth, but he can't snarl or growl 'cause Vor's one-thou-sand-and-one guards will hear him and kill him for entering my quarters. Dani gave me a tour of the palace in which she said my room is the most guarded space in the building because, and I quote, *Mae is most precious to the Ra tribe.*

Growing up, I slept in attics, even a basement once, but mainly shared rooms with other kids (biological kids in the house who seldom liked me in their spaces), so I never quite felt precious enough to have my own room, let alone the entire upper floor of the palace. I guess, now that I think about it, it's also an attic, albeit a spacious, cool one.

Ark dips his head, his beard prickling my cheek, the heat of his body pressing against me almost painfully. Aggression rolls off him in waves, and he smells like the forest and sandalwood, as if he rolled in dirt before he came here. But he didn't. He's clean. Always smells both fresh and heavy, like the forest after rain. And dirty like sex.

"Hello again, Mae."

I mumble beneath his palm on my mouth, then try to knee him again, but he grips my leg and lifts it higher and over his hip. Mischief dances in his eyes when he says, "Now the other leg, and you're all spread and ready."

I narrow my eyes, wishing I could shoot daggers out of them.

"Make noises, alert anyone to my presence, and I'll bind you, then gag you with my cock for the rest of the night. Understood?"

I narrow my eyes into slits. Where is the heat and fire now, hm, Mae? *Burn him!*

"Nod your pretty head," he says.

Oh, he thinks my head is pretty. Coming from his mouth, that's a compliment. I'll take it. I nod, and he releases me, but doesn't step away, his body still pressed up against mine. He's breathing heavily, silver eyes on my mouth, and as if on command, I part my lips.

"I can smell Vor on you."

"And he will smell you on me tomorrow."

"Not if you bathe."

"I'm not bathing with you here."

"What *will* you do with me here?" His breath brushes my lips. He's so close, teasing me, making me want to rip all my clothes off and let him fuck me against the door. Nope, not gonna happen.

Ark's nostrils flare, and a purr rises in his chest. Between his legs, he grows hard. Immediately, he steps away and narrows his eyes. "I never knew Mae was one of the seducers."

"Me either." I fix my clothes and hair and lift my chin, but I still whisper because, well, be it as it may, I enjoy Ark's company and I'd like it if he stayed the night. Tomorrow, my life will change forever into a life of fake friendships and relationships. I sure fucking hope I know how to fake orgasms in case I can't get it up for Vor.

But Ark? He's real. He speaks his mind.

After the night we shared back when he was hurt, I feel like a bond formed between us. It's probably just me who feels that way, and it's probably for the best because Vor secured my vote already.

In a way, rejecting Ark now is an act of self-preservation, and as my sister mentioned when she spoke of Ark, *Why would I pick a soldier when I can pick a future king?* Vor's gonna be the Ra king. Dani will secure his position. Ark's days, or as the predators would call them, spans, are numbered. However, I won't be the one to tell him that.

"What are you doing here?" I ask.

"Ensuring my victory, of course. What else would I be doing here?"

I snort and walk to my armoire. Yes, I have an armoire. It's glorious, with an entire chest of jewels all my own. "You're too late. This chest assured my pick for day one." The chest, Dani said, belonged to Mae, the goddess whose spirit lives inside me. My acceptance of the gift was a pledge saying I would pick Vor as the day one winner of the games.

It's not as if I had a choice. I accepted the chest because Dani offered it, and one doesn't say no to Dani. You either accept or you face the consequences. I've seen her slay people with that crooked smile, a single-tilt-to-the-left smile.

There's a single-tilt-to-the-right smile too, but that's for a different purpose.

"You took coins from me before you took a bribe from him. Or did Vor's dick erase your memory?"

I yank the bindings that hold up my hair, and as my hair falls, I massage my scalp. Wearing my hair up and either tightly braided or pinned weighs heavily on my head. "I haven't seen Vor's dick yet, but I'm sure it can make me forget about you."

Ark falls on the plush pillows and furs by the fireplace, and one flame leans toward him as he sprawls next to it on his side, one knee up, elbow supporting his weight on one arm. He plays with the black stone on one of the large golden rings he wears, circling it around the finger with his thumb. "His dick can't make you forget me." Ark pauses. "Or my coins."

It's annoying how conceited (and right) he is. And how he plays with words is even more annoying. The conversation was about the coins, not him as a person, and I gave myself away. Subtly, but I did it. I swear to God, Ark inherited some of his mother's clarity. Every word is measured with great care, and every word is used to advance the cause.

With a huff, I turn away and face the mirror so I can see to unwind my hair. The predator females fix it so that it lasts for days. I can go to war with this hairdo, and not a single strand's gonna come out of its place. Leather is woven into a giant braid, then secured with more leather. I'm trying to find the end of it all, following tiny knots, hoping one of them will give way for the row and release my hair, when I catch Ark rising from the furs and approaching me.

Christ, he doesn't walk like a man. He stalks the way a panther might, even when he's not trying to look threatening.

Ark takes one of my braids between his fingertips, and

with the flick of a claw, releases the small braid, which loosens the entire hair. "Niz and Kari braided your hair in what we call a Kas skon im style."

Suddenly, I'm annoyed he knows the two predator females Dani assigned to me. They're both beautiful and gentle, and I have no idea why all that even matters.

Ark continues, "The name comes from the Ka tribe. It's the original way their females used to braid their hair."

"I thought you hated the Ka."

"We do. Or, we did. Some of us. It's complicated."

The Ra have warred with the Ka since the beginning of time. "Why would the Ra braid my hair in Ka style?"

"Because Ka was the name of Mae's lover." Ark stands at my side, his ierto brushing my arm. If I lifted my hand, I could grab his sac. Not gonna do that right now, but just thinking about it makes me want to laugh. Or masturbate. I can't make up my mind.

"Since Mae's daughter," Ark says, voice low and raspy because he can purr and speak at the same time (it's masturbate), "the goddess of thunder and pain, tried to seduce Mae's husband and failed. The daughter grew angry at his refusal and then went off to form her own tribe named the Ka. But before all that, the Ra and Ka were one tribe united under one goddess, Mae, who birthed many strong predators and most importantly, predator females. Ka, the lover, would braid her hair," Ark pauses before saying, "like this." He removes the leathers holding my hair, and immediately, the tension in my head releases. I press my fingernails into my scalp for a massage while Ark grabs a brush. He twirls it in his hand, a small smile playing on his lips.

Tonight, his eyes are white, that of a male, not silver, those of his hunter. Ark's rarely this relaxed or calm. I like him most when we're alone. It reminds me of the night we shared when he was hurt.

"I like your people's stories," I tell him.

"I know."

"How would you know that?"

"Tash told me."

I face him. "When?" I miss Imani, the good mom I never had, even Tash, the sexy warlord who ought to have kidnapped me and run off with me instead of Imani, but that's the grudge I'll hold in silence for the rest of my life with Vor. I don't crush on Tash. I crush on the thought of how good Imani and Tash are with each other. I want one of those good males. That's all. Nobody can blame a girl for wanting to spend her life with a good male.

"When I saw him last." Ark ruffles up my hair. "Where the fuck is it?" Ark whisper-hisses.

"Huh?"

"The fucking script."

I stare blankly at him.

He takes out the comb holding the back of my hair up and examines it. He pauses and breaks the comb.

"Hey!" I shout.

Ark's ears twitch.

A knock comes from the other side of the door. That's the guard letting me know he's there if I need him.

"I'm fine," I say. "Just trying to untangle my hair."

"The Kas style," the guard says. "Third knot on the fourth braid above the ear should do it."

Oh, there's a method to the madness. "Thank you for that, Lez."

"Anytime, Mae."

Ark's listening and tilts his head, then he says, "Why do you know the guard's name?"

"Because I introduced myself."

"If he is competing tomorrow, I'll kill him right after I kill Vor."

"Kill Vor? No." I shake my head. "You can't do that."

Ark preens like an offended peacock. "I can."

"I'm not questioning your fitness."

"Then why shouldn't I kill him?"

"Because he's your brother."

"So?"

"So you're family."

"Again. So?"

"Would you kill Tash?"

Ark lifts an eyebrow.

I sigh. He tried to kill Tash once already, but that was under Bera's influence, though I'm unsure how much of that is an excuse and how much of it is Ark's thirst for violence. "If Vor dies, your mother will go on a murderous rampage."

"If she's still breathing."

"She's your mother, and for all her faults, she's made sure I'm well cared for." I can't say the same for another "mother" who took me into her house.

"Besides, Ark"—I clear my throat—"I like Vor. He's nice to me."

Ark smirks. "The problem is, human, Mae picked me, and you know it."

"I do not," I lie.

"Fine. I will remind you." Ark slams his mouth over mine and takes me back to the night we spent together, the night I fell in love with a predator.

CHAPTER FOUR

LENA

Ma *onths ago, the night after Ark tried to kill his*
brother Tash...

∼

On Tash's property, nestled in a meadow, stands a small one-story home made of stacked rock. Before entering Ark's house, I pause to touch a few rocks near the door, trying to push one to see if the whole thing might collapse. It doesn't.

Cool. I have a hard time believing Ark would have the patience and smarts to build a house like this made entirely of rocks stacked on top of one another. I'm pretty sure he made it, though. These predators take great pride in their ability to live self-sustainably.

The door, made of gray, blue, and black pebbles, appears almost like an ancient mosaic, an art piece, really, and it must've taken years to make. I poke a pebble, again trying to see if it'll move, then peek between the rocks to see if these pebbles are glued together. Doesn't seem like they are.

A growl comes from inside. Ark hears me lingering out

here. Predators hear and see better than humans because of the animal they can shift into. They don't like to think of themselves as animals, but we, the humans, do. We call their kind predators, a dual-form alien that has one animal and one male form. They predate on humans. After our crash, they stole our pods and forced us to live on their planet.

"I'm coming in," I say and push open the door.

One of my foster moms (there've been so many, I can't remember which one) let a wounded stray dog into the yard. She sent me to bring the dog water, and it bit me. I still have a scar over my thumb. Lesson learned was that wounded animals bite.

Ark's wounded. I know I shouldn't walk into his lair and close the door behind me, especially not when he's lying in the corner on top of the furs, eyeing me with his one good eye, the other hanging out of its socket.

His bloody muzzle exposes sharp canines, each the size of my finger. Blood drips from his mouth, and he swipes a tongue over it, purring as if telling me he likes the taste of it. He does. Ark likes to bleed others. He's always picking a fight and saying whatever is on his mind, which usually pisses off his tribemates. That's his brother's blood he's swallowing.

I dislike that he's still in hunter form and can't talk. Hunters are animals, always hungry and prone to violence. "Wanna know what I'm thinking?" I ask, still from the door. My heart's pounding, fear that he might snap and attack me a constant reminder that he's a predator and I'm the prey.

Ark growls.

"I like it when you can't talk."

Ark growls louder, the sound of it making me want to release my bladder. Nervously, I giggle. "Imani sent me," I say and take a step toward him, pausing when he lifts his head. His eye, hanging by a thread from the socket, swings, and I look away. Gross.

"Said I should stay with you."

Ark's watching me, but has stopped growling, so I approach and kneel on the fur near him. My palms sweat, and I'm so scared that I want to throw up, but I can't leave. It's like a compulsion.

Something's sticking to my knee. I stand back up. The blood, either his brother's or his, has soaked the fur. "You should probably lie on something other than your bed." I swipe two fingers over the blood and lift them to show him.

Ark tilts his head, eye on my lifted two fingers. With a grunt, he stands and wobbles toward the middle of the room. A hatch opens, and the ground shakes for a second to reveal a secret underground passage.

"Oooo," I whisper and peek down. This is so creepy. I've always loved creepy things. I think it's curiosity. Better than thinking of myself as a reckless dumbass, in any case.

There're no stairs and the fall's steep, but I can make it without breaking my legs or neck. I think. I jump, land, slide on my side, and hit the ground with my hip. Grunting, I stand and look up to see if Ark caught that. I hate when he sees me tripping around Tash's property, because he always laughs. I'm fairly clumsy and he's…a lithe and agile asshole who makes fun of me whenever he feels like it.

Hmm, he's not up there.

Oh no, is this a trap? Is he gonna close the exit above me? Fuck, I *am* a reckless dumbass.

Ark lands right in front of me.

I scream and scramble backward, trip over something, and eat shit on my back, legs up over my body. Might as well do a fucking cartwheel. Somehow, I untangle my limbs and stand, fixing my hair and all. Ark's on two feet, so he can speak now.

"You scared the shit out of me!" I scream.

Ark shows me his teeth. "Don't care." He walks forward,

and I walk back until my spine hits the stone. Only too late, I realize he's cornered me. Predators love doing that. Cornering their prey. They think this is normal behavior between a nude male and a dressed female, but it's not, and I won't have it. I jut out my chin, his hanging eyeball distracting me from telling him to fuck off and put on some clothes.

"You should take care of that eye."

"Put it back in."

I shake my head. His body's touching mine. I smell him. I smell his aggression, blood, madness, animal, all of it, and part of me wants to climb him like a tree, while the other part of me (you know, the sane one) wants to push him away. I opt for neither and carry on a conversation. "I'm not touching it."

"Bera sent you to care for me, so that's what you'll do."

"Imani asked me to come here, not Bera."

Ark snorts. "Same difference. Put the fucking eye back in."

"You put the eye back in."

"No."

"Why not?" I ask.

"Because that's what you're gonna do."

I gag. "You can't pay me to pick up that eye." I'm not trying to be a bitch. I'm so grossed out. I'm the girl who vomits when others are vomiting. Couldn't be a nurse if I wanted to, not that I know what I want anyway. It's not nursing, I know that much, and Imani asked me to be a nurse to him.

"There's a price for everything," he says. "And I can pay."

Hmm. We're going to the market soon, and I have no money and no way to earn it around here. Tash paid last time, and while that's lovely, I'd like to earn my keep.

Ark smiles. "You're going to Ralna's market, I hear. You will need coins for nice things. You like nice things."

Fucker knows. I do love nice things, namely jewelry and expensive fine fabrics. I love nice things because I could never have them until now, until Tash bought me beautiful jewels and clothes, things that belong to me and only me, things that nobody had used before, not other kids in the house or strangers from thrift shops or even my older sister.

"How do you know what I like?" I ask.

"Because I have eyes, and I watch."

"You don't have eyes anymore. Only one eye." I smile back. Got ya! Ha. Finally.

"Fix me so I have my two eyes." He steps back and whines, then holds his lower back. He's in pain, although it's difficult to ascertain that because he bears it so well. Yet just because he bears it well doesn't mean it doesn't hurt. I have to remember that. Sighing, I say, "Okay."

Ark rolls his shoulders, then slaps his palms against the wall around my head. "Do it."

His face is inches from mine, and I'm trying not to focus on the empty eye socket, thinking that if I put back his eye, it'll fill the bloody void.

When I don't move, he grabs my wrist and guides my hand to the eye. Swallowing, I take it between my fingers. "Gross." It's slimy. "This won't work. You can't just fit it back into place."

"It can, and you will."

Sweat beads my forehead as my hand travels to the empty socket, Ark's eyeball between my fingertips. Ark's watching me, his one-eyed gaze unnerving.

"Your hand is shaking," he says.

"You make me nervous."

"I'm the one who's gonna lose the eye if you don't put it back in soon."

"It doesn't grow back or something?"

"It'll dry out and fall off. What's your problem?"

I align the eye with the socket. All I have to do is push it in. "Should I push it in slowly or hard?"

"Hmmm. I don't know. My first time with this kind of injury."

"Pick one," I say.

"Slowly," he whispers and leans in an inch while using the grip on my wrist to move my arm and guide the eye back where it belongs. Ark blinks and rolls the orb, and for some reason, I expect it to turn the white of a man's, but it remains the silver of his animal. The color of his other eye, the one that's not repairing, is white. Ark's eyes are mostly always silver, his hunter always ready to pounce, but tonight, the eyes don't match.

"Well done, Lena."

My breath hitches. I didn't even think he knew my name, and I'm certain he's never addressed me directly before. His dual-colored eyes lock with mine, and suddenly, I realize we're alone, in his lair, underground. A male and a female. He's nude, pressing me against the wall, and my flimsy little robe lacks the thread count to prevent me from feeling the draw of his hard body.

"Fuck me," he purrs.

"I don't want to."

"A lie," he says, and trails his nose down my cheek, inhaling my scent. "Your smell invites me to take a bite." He licks my cheek, stops by my jugular, and nips, his belly growling. "It also invites me to seed you. I can't say I've ever wanted to seed a female before, but I don't question my instincts. Come, I want to fuck you."

"No."

"Yes."

I push his chest, but he won't budge. He licks my cheek, again making his belly rumble.

Past his shoulder, a flame ignites in the pit.

Ark spins and presses me against the wall. I peek around his broad body to see the flame detach from the base of the pit and hover in the air above it. Ark drops to his knees, and I stand there staring at the weird-ass shit that is the fire hovering in the air. The single flame travels over to him and hovers above him until Ark throws back his head. Eyes closed, he spreads his arms and opens his mouth to swallow the flame.

Minutes pass.

"Ark?" I whisper.

"Mae," he answers me.

CHAPTER FIVE

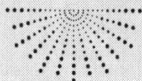

LENA

*I*n my short twelve-year career as a student, I've changed seventeen schools, and day one of the games feels like the first day in a new school. On the first day, I'm always a nervous mess. A throwing-up kind of mess. Even now, and even when Dani is eyeballing me with those big white eyes that look like golf balls, I'm vomiting bile into the bath.

With a bored look on her face, one of my servants hands me a small cloth, and I wipe my mouth with it.

Dani gets her shocked shit together (I'm sure this female never had a nerve-racking day in her life) and sighs. "For most females, anxiety on the day of the games is normal."

"Were you nervous on your game day?"

Dani's eyelids drop just a fraction, and she looks at the floor as if remembering. She smiles with both edges of her mouth lifted. It softens her features, and she says, "Not that I can recall."

And there ya have it. Just when I thought I'd reached that deeply hidden soft center of this predator female, she proves me wrong.

"I was excited," she continues. "Perhaps you're excited and not nervous. There's a difference, you know."

"I know."

"You must be exited, then," she states firmly.

"Yes, ma'am," I say.

Dani nods in approval and dismisses the servant with a flick of her wrist as if she's shooing off annoying flies. Her scent, a lilac flower called lanever, I believe, pleasant and inviting, precedes her as she approaches me. From a pouch strapped onto her wrist, right next to a dagger, she pulls out a bracelet. At the center of it is an unrefined stone, white and milky with tiny blue starlike dots inside it. It reminds me of the sea when the moon hits the surface.

"It's beautiful," I say.

"It is a family stone passed on to me by my mother. The stone passes calming energy into one's body. No more of that wretched display of weakness."

"Any one weakness, or all the weaknesses?" I ask as she fastens the bracelet around my left wrist.

"The vomiting, dear."

"Ah," I comment. "How is Vor?"

She smiles, eyes flashing the silver of her huntress. "My son is well prepared."

"I'm happy to hear that."

"And even if he wasn't, he's ensured his victory."

"For sure."

Dani nods. "I am pleased."

"Happy to please." I nod. "Always. At your service, ma'am, yes, ma'am."

She's staring at me, clearly not quite knowing if I'm fucking with her or if I'm serious. Bit of both.

Sometimes I'll say shit just to irritate her. It pleases me when I can do that. Passive aggression I think is the term for what I'm doing, and I like it. No way would I dare confront this crazy female head-on.

"You are ready," she states, not asking if I am. I better be.

The second Dani pulls back the blinds and opens the massive double doors leading to the terrace that extends out to the middle of the roof, which I've never before stepped foot onto, my belly rises and I bend over the bath once more and gag into the water. Clutching the bracelet she gave me, I wait for the spinning in my head to subside, and when it doesn't, I think I might faint.

Ever since the cruiser bound for Joylius exploded and I traveled in a tiny pod through space, I've feared heights something fierce. While I live at the top of the castle with a blazing fire coming from the roof, beautiful richly colored fabrics cover the windows, which I don't open. I didn't even know about the terrace. The door to it is seamlessly fitted into the rest of the roof, and frankly, I wouldn't have thought that there would be an exit on a slanted part of the room.

Out on the terrace, Dani's retreating figure moves toward the rails. She's not waiting for me or walking with me, but instead expecting me to follow her.

As I walk, my head spins, making me sway on my feet. It's loud as fuck on the terrace. Predators in the city shout as Dani waves, then turns her head, giving me her profile, telling me with small gestures that I need to be next to her. If she has to turn and call me, I'll get in trouble.

But my head spins.

Bile is rising in my throat.

My knees are growing weak, threatening to fold.

I was so excited about the games, and now I'm a wreck. It's not so much the games. The height's got me. It feels like I'm standing at the top of the world. Figuratively, that's fun. Literally, not so much. Imani used to calm me when I'd get this freaked out. She would tell me to focus on my breathing. I find and identify items around me that I can pick up and control.

I breathe though my nose, long deep breaths, and glance around. Torches burn on both sides of me. The roof is always on fire. It's the energy from Mae, their goddess. Me. The fire invites me to look, to move it, to feel the burning on my skin. My hand, as if not my own, extends, fingertips reaching for the flame at the top of the torch.

The fire hops from the torch to the top of my hand. I freak out and scream, pulling back my hand, thinking it's gonna burn me. The flame drops onto my beautiful white dress and sets it ablaze.

Oh my fuck! I start blowing at it, stomping, dancing, running around the terrace like a chicken with her head cut off, but nope, the dress is on fire and the fire is spreading upward. I'm gonna burn to ashes.

I run back inside the room and prepare to jump into the bath, but my body freezes.

"No," sounds in my head.

It's a command my body obeys. My feet, as if they're someone else's, walk away from the water and back toward the terrace to stand next to Dani.

The dress burns brightly. The fire is spreading quickly, reaching my trunk, arms, neck, face until it turns the dress into ashes that fly around me. Only then does it die down.

There's a moment of silence where time seems to stop and I can collect myself long enough to breathe. Below the terrace, the predators fill the streets. Past the city, miles and miles of them have come for the games. The silence of so many people makes me want to puke again.

I don't know if I'm supposed to say anything. I caught fire and didn't burn.

"I'm sorry about the dress, Dani." It was her mother's dress, beautiful, with precious stones woven into the white leather ierto that extended into a corset on the top. When she doesn't respond, I glance at her.

Dani's pale, and the look of shock on her face is undeniable.

"I feel the same way," I tell her.

I stand there, now mortified to be naked in front of the city of Ralna, which is filled with what seems like half the population of the Ra tribe that have come to witness the games.

Dani grips my hand and squeezes harder than she should. I press my lips together lest I scream in pain. I try jerking it away, but she holds tight.

"It seems," she utters though gritted teeth, her lopsided smile in place, "Mae wasn't pleased with the dress." She releases my hand, and I fist my fingers and relax my hand again to make sure the predator female didn't break any bones.

"I'm sorry about the dress," I repeat.

"Get ahold of yourself, human."

"I'm trying."

"Try harder." Dani waves. "The rumors of human females carrying our goddesses are now confirmed as true," she announces, her voice measured and authoritative. "Mae has returned home."

People start chanting a prayer I've heard many times before. Actually, it's a prayer every tribe member on the planet chants right before they throw in the herbs or blood or whatever sacrifice they intended to make when starting a fire. It lasts only a few seconds before the males cheer and shout, and I hear a single word repeated: "Games, games, games!"

It puts a smile on my face. Games. I like watching sports.

Dani lifts an arm to silence the crowds, but Vor appears next to me and pecks me on the cheek before standing by me instead of his mother. The males boo him, and he laughs, and I smile wider. However, Dani isn't amused. She stares daggers at me.

I need to wake the fuck up and humble down, get off Dani's stage, which is the terrace now. She hates sharing the throne, the stage, and definitely power over her people. I feel like if it were up to her, she'd be up here alone, and we mere mortals would be down below, looking up at her and obeying her whims.

Trouble is, I don't think Mae, the goddess, listens to mere mortals like Dani, and I have a feeling Mae set my body on fire and burned the dress on purpose. Mae might also cost me my life, so Dani's advice to get hold of myself is one I ought to heed.

Vor holds my hand and gently, almost seductively, rubs his thumb over my palm. He is wearing black on black, his face painted half charcoal, half red. The males below start passing on the paint and smearing it on their bodies and faces, even on their weapons. I turn toward Vor, and he lifts our connected hands, showing me he's smeared red paint on my palm with his thumb. He lifts my palm to the masses, and they boo him again. Metal starts clashing against metal as a male I recognize approaches. His name is Feli, and he won, then mated one of my friends.

"Hi, Feli," I greet him.

He nods and almost trips over his feet as he steps onto an empty raised platform just on my right.

Dani whips her head around and glares at me.

Uh-oh. I swallow. "Sorry?"

She shakes her head. "I see my son hasn't briefed you on game etiquette."

"She greeted a mated male," Vor says.

"Your father was also mated, and I took him without a greeting. Keep that in mind, son."

Vor clears his throat and addresses me. "You mustn't show favor to any one male unless you intend for him to win. They're all watching for favors. The one you favor will be the targeted male in the games."

"That would be you, then," I lie.

He smiles, showing me all his teeth. There's blood on one of them, and he licks it off with his tongue. "Indeed."

"Luckily for my son, he has nothing to worry about since he's the fittest male to enter the games, with plenty of friends who owe us favors also competing. In the end, you will pick him. All this is just for our people to have some fun. Everyone knows who the winner will be." She pins me with a pointed look.

"Yes, ma'am." I nod. "Understood."

Dani cups my cheeks. "You've chosen wisely, human."

My cheeks heat up, and Dani jerks her hands away. She stares at her burned palms, then fists them at her sides, plastering a neutral expression on her face.

Oh my fuck, I think the goddess just burned her. She threw up heat on my cheeks and burned Dani. Holy crap, is Mae trying to kill me? She and I need to have a conversation, which should be interesting seeing as I'll have to talk to myself.

A roar sounds behind us, and I spin to see the fire on the roof shoot to life, reaching impossible heights.

The predators shout, and Feli starts moving his arms over what I'm sure is a game control center. I remember him doing this during my sister's games back on Tash's property. I can't see the portals or the portal controls, but I know they're there.

Feli starts rattling off names, starting with Vor, who, at

the sound of his name, pecks my cheek again and hops off the terrace and down several rails until he reaches the group of males I most often see him with. They pat him on the shoulder, and I lean over—slightly!—to see him better. He looks up and blows me a kiss.

I do the same, but my gaze doesn't linger on him. I search the crowd while the fire on the roof keeps roaring, while the crowds below keep getting more and more restless as they anticipate the competition and bloodshed.

Thousands of people stand near the palace. I can't sift through them all, and Feli's rattling off the names of males, none of whom is the one I want to hear. I wring my hands and keep searching, my palm starting to heat up, melting the bracelet Dani gave me. "Stop that," I hiss at myself, wanting to quit generating so much heat. The pretty bracelet melts, and I peel it off my skin, wondering how I'm gonna hide the fact that I destroyed it. Fuck. Dani will definitely kill me.

A cool wind blows our way and makes me shiver. I'm still nude and should be shivering and shy, wanting to cover up, but on the inside, my body burns like those fires on the roof. He's not coming.

Feli announces the games closed at max capacity.

The predators cheer.

Dani sighs what I could swear is a breath of relief.

I step closer to the terrace's edge, my eyes everywhere at once.

"Are you looking for me?" A whisper at my ear.

I spin and lie, "No."

Ark is wearing a white ierto with white belts decorated in painted black metal and studs. His uniform is crisp and new, his plush lips painted white and red. Two long bird feathers, one blue and one white, dangle from his ears all the way down to the middle of his chest. Without thinking about it, I stroke the blue one, and as if compelled, I say, "Real Om feathers."

"Mmhm," he says.

"Why is your name not on that list, predator?"

Ark chuckles, his silver eyes lifting at the corners. "I'm late." He unties the top of his belt and reveals four stab wounds. Blood oozes out of one, and I come to my senses and cover my mouth with a hand. "Oh my God, you need to get that checked." *Stupid, Lena. They self-heal.*

Ark slides his silver gaze to Dani. "Hello, Mother. You seem shocked to see me."

Dani smiles back like a shark. "You are late."

"You kept me busy."

What's that mean?

"I am only looking out for you, son. You have no friends left here. Go back to skulking around the lands and leave Ralna to its rightful heir."

Ark purses his lips. "I would have had you not decided to hold the games for Mae in Ralna. Your mistake, not mine. Tash was happy to host her games."

"Mae belongs here with us."

"I couldn't agree more."

"She has picked her predator."

Ark smiles like a shark. He gets that from his mother. Holy crap, these two are the same. Hate's rolling off them in waves, but to an outsider, this would look like a normal conversation, as if mother and son are briefly at odds, but nothing too dangerous. I know better.

Dani will do anything she can to kill Ark in the games. She likely sent predators after him and that's how he got those stab wounds, and that's why he was late.

"I'm aware of who she picked," Ark says. "Nevertheless, my spot in the games is guaranteed."

"We are at full capacity," Feli interjects. "Four hundred males."

Ark winks. "That's why I signed up first."

Feli frowns and appears to read the screen before him. "You *are* on the list."

"Told you," Ark says, and like Vor, he hops onto the railing, but then swipes a hand and jumps into an open pocket of air. He disappears.

"What the hell was that, Feli?" Dani hisses.

"I don't know."

"Find out!"

"Over here," Ark shouts from the top of the merchant's cart at one corner of the busy market. He holds up something dark and round. "These are portal pockets." He hops off the cart and into thin air and reappears behind Dani.

She spins, hands fisted.

"I can move in and out of any place without a portal base," he says. "As for the games, Mother, it pays to be friends with the Ka. Their portal master is an asset. He can hack anything, including your games. Careful, Mother, the entire Ka army could pop up here any moment now."

Dani snorts, not ladylike at all, so that tells me he's getting to her. He pisses her off. Hell, Ark can piss off anyone.

"The Ka won't save you," she says. "Arriving here alone is stupid. Your arrogance will cost you a win."

Briefly, Ark glances at me, then back at his mother. He smiles, a single tilt at the corner of his lips. "Let's play, Mother."

"Let's," Dani hisses. "I look forward to seeing the look on your face when she picks my son."

Ark winces, but shows Dani his teeth. "Three spans!" he shouts.

"Two nights," Dani announces.

They look at me. "One…" Fuck, I forgot the rest. "Dude?" It can't be dude.

"One winner," Vor shouts from below.

Nice save. I smile at him.

He winks.

I wink back. Pleased, Dani strokes my hair. "Good girl."

Woof woof.

CHAPTER SIX

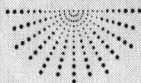

ARK

*D*uring Mae's sister's games on Tash's property, where I competed for fun and out of obligation to my people, I lurked by the lake while the human females bathed. Before I knew she was a goddess, I used to spend the entire morning by the lake, waiting for the young female to arrive and take off her clothes.

She stands nude on the terrace, so I shouldn't be staring at her. I've seen all her assets already.

It's just that now, I'm annoyed everyone else has seen them too, even though nudity is to be expected from Mae, seeing as she's ill-tempered and burns though her clothes when she's angry.

The human Mae inhabited is also a bit hot-tempered, and I delighted in her setting my mother's game-day dress on fire. The dress's ashes still linger on the terrace, which brings a smile to my face.

It's about the only thing that does bring a smile to my face this span.

I woke up all the way in the corner of Ka territory in a puddle of my own blood, dying of wounds I don't remember receiving. I also don't remember how I got to the Ka territory or how those three dismembered Ka males I found lying around me died. I sure as fuck didn't kill them. Not that that's gonna matter when Hart, the Kai of the Ka tribe, finds my blood near their bodies. But I'll worry about Hart later.

Now, I have more important things to do, such as win span one of the games, which means I have to survive and deliver a gift for Mae.

Although my ally, Feli, monitors the games, the second the contestants clear out, my mother will send him off on a fool's errand and take over the controls. Mother hides most of her talents, and being a portal master is one such talent. She is one of the brightest tribal members, with the wisdom of her age. It's unfortunate she's also my biggest enemy and my brother Vor is her muscle. And my competition when it comes to winning the human on the terrace.

Feli's eyes find mine as my mother approaches him, practically gliding over the terrace as if Eme, goddess of grace, inhabited her. The male bends his head so my mother can whisper in his ear. Moments later, Feli leaves and my mother flexes her fingers, an evil smile on her face. My tribemates, mainly her allies, groan.

I scrub my beard and curse under my breath.

The games are gonna be brutal, especially for me.

Spatial openings pop up all over Ralna, but the males fail to rush into the portals. They're not stomping all over each other and getting a head start. Only their weapons are drawn, their eyes on me, waiting for me to jump into a portal so they can follow and eliminate me.

I laugh. "Vor!" I shout. "I think the people identified me as the most dangerous threat. That ought to tell you something. Mainly, you're not it." I search the crowd for my little stepbrother and find I've lost sight of him. This pisses me off.

Mae's fine tits distracted me, and now I'm gonna walk right into an ambush.

The bleeding wounds from the daggers that almost pierced my heart mean my blood is coating air that's already thick with violence and the competitive spirits of my people.

Inhaling loudly, I crack my neck and bend at the knees. A portal opens, and I jump inside, popping in near the portal that leads to Folor Observatory. Turning, I grab for the portal controls inside and try to close it so no more of my people can enter. I realize Mother has blocked my closing capabilities just as males start pouring into the clearing. I leave the portal station and sprint across the island, barely having any memory of the layout.

The last time I was here, I was six. My father dropped me off. The observatory used to be one of his safe houses during the wars, and I wonder why Mother opened this space for the tribe.

At full speed, I run through the thick forest toward the safe house, praying I remember the way. I know Mother sent me here on purpose, just as I know she arranged those three dead Ka males this morning. I don't know if I killed them. I don't know how she plans to kill me.

Knowing she does, however, is motivation enough to keep me running, oozing blood from my wounds and giving away my position. I can't hole up and hide.

Mother is telling me without telling me that she knows I've hidden on this island before and that no place on the Ra land is safe for me. If she knows about this remote location, she's likely uncovered the other three Tash and I have killed to keep secret. I hope I fucking live long enough to at least tell him our locations have been compromised.

My wounds are slowing me down.

Behind me, I hear the crunch of leaves under my tribe-mates' boots.

The males won't stop until they've killed me. My mother will execute them if they return without my head. Or maybe Mother would like to have my canines. A claw? My bleeding fucking heart, likely. She'd feed it to Vor and Mae's baby.

Holy Herea, I'm all gloomy thoughts and bad spirits this span.

I break through the forest and continue running, nearing the cliff. Tash and I camped here once, two logs and a firepit still standing. I rush past them toward the cliff, take out the spatial disruptor sphere, and turn it left toward the observatory in the middle of the seas.

Before I escape, I turn and wave at the several dozen males chasing me. Two of them even run in hunter. Nice! I outran their hunters.

I throw the sphere that creates a portal pocket and jump inside.

The portal spits me out at the base of the observatory. The winds rock the tall, thin, awkward, old metal structure, making my boots slip on the water. My feet are dancing so I don't fall on my face, when claws close over my throat and a dagger stabs my right side under the lung. Pain slices through my brain, and I grunt, holding back a scream. I try spinning, then elbowing him, but can't move. Vor's holding me tightly by the back of my neck while I hold his hand by the wrist so he can't rip into me and tear out my lungs.

He spins me so my side is to his front.

Silver eyes stare back at me, and his sneer makes me smile. Blood seeps from the corner of my mouth. The winds rock the observatory. Our feet are unsteady, and we are either both gonna fall into the sea or I'm gonna die.

I think I'll die anyway. Might as well take my little brother with me.

I grab the back of his neck and head butt him, breaking his nose. Blood gushes out of it and onto my face, and I taste it, marveling at the tang of it. My hunter, thirsty for more inside my head, whines, begging me to attack my brother.

But Vor fighting me in male makes me think he believes he can outmatch me on two feet, and that just won't do. The games are designed so that the fittest predator wins the prize.

Vor slips, and I seize the split-second opportunity and yank the dagger out of my side with a roar. I throw his weapon away, followed by all of mine. Well, all that he can see. I still have a few stashed away here and there on my person.

"Come here, mama's boy," I call, trying to get a steady footing for when he attacks.

Vor takes hold of a rope attached to the observatory tower. This stabilizes him while I'm still rocking on the base structure, which heaves with the waves.

"You want to live?" Vor asks, wiping seawater from his face, then taking a vial from his ierto pocket. It's got a purple or maybe pink solution inside. I can't tell the color. I can barely see from the pain, and my vision is blurring. Gonna pass out and drown in the sea. What a pathetic way for a predator to die.

"The wounds won't heal, Ark. Take the anse serum and this parcel of the land, and never come back."

The males who stabbed me (I'm doubting it's the three dead Ka males now) coated their daggers with orda, a poisonous secretion from the ortain plant. Anse plant secretions negate the poison. Neither of those plants is lawfully grown, and even if they were, they're imports from tribes we have no alliance with. Things have changed in Ralna, and I remained in the dark because Mother has killed every spy I sent to her court.

"She wants to make a deal?" Mother offered to spare my life. I'm touched. Really.

Orda poison spreads slowly and kills even more slowly, but death is inevitable. I need the antidote, but I'm too weak to take it from Vor.

Pretending as if I slipped, I fall into the sea. Cold water seeps into my very bones, and as a hunter, I hate being wet. Still, I battle the waves and swim to the other side of the observatory where the waves are not hitting the structure and the water is calmer. Under the water, I lurk and watch as Vor enters the observatory tower and appears at the tiny window at the top of the tower, searching the seas for me. He can't see me, and I barely see him.

My head pokes out so my nose is up above the waves.

Vor tucks the vial into his inner ierto pocket and turns away, disappearing for a few moments, enough time for me to emerge and not drown. But I don't follow him yet, not until I home in on his footsteps.

I listen. He's still at the top, so I jump on the base, throw a sphere, and direct my spatial jump toward his position.

I materialize before a stunned Vor and punch him in the face. He flies back, in midair already preparing to land on his feet. I jump and kick him, sending his body flying into the metal wall. His head bangs against the side of it, and I hear a crack. I hope that was his skull and not the vial I need.

Vor wipes the blood from his temple, then reaches for the vial and pulls it out. I try to snatch it, but he moves faster than I do.

"I'll break it before I let you have the antidote," he says.

"She will kill you, Vor."

"Mae?"

Huh. Look at that. He has doubts about Mae. Why else bring her up? I wasn't thinking Mae, I was thinking our mother, but I go with whatever Vor started. "Mmhm."

Vor shakes his head as if to clear it. I rattled his brains. Bet his vision is as blurry as mine. *Nice going, Ark. Keep it up, and don't die in the process.* My dick won't work if I'm dead. Or poisoned, which reminds me. I need that antidote.

"It's not up to Mae," he says. "It's up to Lena, and she hates you and likes me."

I'm hating how he's saying her name. It's almost a whisper, a bit too intimate for my taste, and makes me wonder if he bled her virgin pussy before I did. "The human," I bite out, bile rising into my throat, stars playing over my eyes, "is Mae, and Mae favors the fittest."

Vor smiles, his eyes flashing the silver of his hunter. "It seems I am the fittest."

He is right. I am unfit, barely standing on my two feet, so I roar and let my hunter take over. Bones crack, and the dagger hole he made under my rib cage widens, making me roar in pain. Energy depleted, I stumble back, unable to call the hunter. The hunter can't emerge now. I've waited too long. The poison will kill me.

Vor crosses his arms over his chest, a clear sign that he's not intimidated. Before leaving, he sizes me up. "You'll die here, and nobody will ever find your body. You will roam the lands as a ghost of my legacy and watch me fill Lena's belly with my pups. Goodbye, brother."

My knees fold, and I slide down the wall. I sit, my legs spread out before me.

I vowed to bleed that pussy or die trying.

It appears I'll die trying.

CHAPTER SEVEN

LENA

*T*ime passes fast when you're having fun. Dani is having fun, though I can't tell you why. It kind of worries me that she's humming before the portal controls while I sit on a chair made of bloody axes and fur. Feli brought it out to the terrace, and he's standing next to me, on guard for hours now.

My belly rumbles and disrupts Dani's humming. She turns, arching an eyebrow. "That noise will die down as soon as the games are over."

Wait, what? "You mean I can't eat during the games?"

"You can, but you will not."

"Um, and why not?"

"Because you can't accept food or water or anything from any male. That includes you, Feli."

In affirmation, he grunts, the only sound that's come out of the male since Dani took over his station.

She could bring me food. Imani and I brought food for my sister during her games. Hell, we had a picnic right there on the platform Tash set up for the games.

God, I miss him. He was kind to me, and I was at ease

around him, never once fearing for my life even though I knew he was a warlord with lots of land in the tribe. The land comes from the war prizes he's won, so he's a fierce warlord who has killed many.

Does Ark own land? Does Vor? "Does Vor own land?" I ask.

Dani whips her head my way and blinks before cutting Feli with a look. I think I hear him whine just before he replaces her at the command center. Dani glides to me, her royal-blue ierto, made of fine silk, making her appear as a fairy godmother who glides over the ground. She's more like that evil stepmother from Snow White than a fairy godmother, but whatever. She ain't no helpless little princess, that's for sure. Am I? Hmmm.

Imani was like a godmother. I miss her too. Her presence gave me courage.

Dani takes my hand and pulls gently. "Come, child."

We walk to the railing, and Dani extends an arm and swipes it over Ralna. "All this is Vor's, the entire city and all the land around the city housing the majority of our tribe. Of course, when he is Rai, all the tribal lands will be his, with all their earldoms, including the goddesses that reside within the earldoms."

Frowning, I'm trying to understand what she's saying, because Dani speaks with purpose. It's up to me to decipher what she really means. "All, as in all the tribal lands?"

Dani nods. "All the tribes shall be united under one king as they were under Mae and her lover, Ka."

Holy fuck, Dani is planning world domination.

"Will the other tribes accept being ruled by one king?"

"Accept? Oh child, Mae needs no permission to rule them all. She is a goddess of fire, blessed and loved by Bera, goddess of war. There is no tribe in the land willing to go to war with either of them, and definitely not with the two of them together."

"Bera is with Tash, whom you tried to sacrifice."

Dani waves a hand. "Bera walks with the Ra, and that's all that matters."

"What about other goddesses? The ones in the Ka tribe."

"I will take care of them." Dani glides closer. "Don't you worry your pretty human head about it." She inhales, practically salivating, and licks her lips. I step back. I am prey, therefore her food, and she must be hungry too, having not eaten all morning.

"Vor will be Rai, and you will have all the pretty dresses and trinkets you desire. You will have all the land." She whispers at my ear, "Including the Ka lands with Aoa, that wretched little bitch who defied Mae and split up the tribes."

Something inside me burns. I glance at the flames over the roof and see they're rising higher.

"You smell delicious." Dani pins me against the rail and nicks my ear with the sharp edge of her tooth.

"Ouch!" I push at her chest and hold my ear, swipe it, and see she's drawn blood. "What the fuck?" I pinch my earlobe to stop the bleeding.

Dani glides back to the portal control.

She bit me and now pretends like nothing happened. A warning bite that if I don't move the way a pawn moves in her game of chess, she's gonna bleed me or find other ways to ensure I do as I'm told. I better behave and let her think she's always in control of me and everything else, including Mae.

That worries me.

I can't control Mae.

And I don't think Mae likes to be controlled. I have a feeling Mae is wild like her fire.

Sitting back in the chair, I swipe my tongue over my dry

lips, prop my hand on an armrest, and think about how I'd like to have my sister around right about now. Or Imani. Or maybe Ark. He takes up all the space in a room and draws people's attention.

Dani would shift her bullshit onto him and leave me alone.

I huff, annoyed that I'm not thinking about having Vor around. He's much nicer than Ark, and also a little more handsome than Ark in a boyish, clean, princely way, not a rough, dirty, and violent Ark way.

Thinking of the devil makes him appear.

Vor strains his muscles as he climbs the railing. He hops over it, then bends, hands on his knees, trying to catch his breath.

Once done surviving the games out there in the wild and retrieving a gift for me, the contestants climb the walls of the palace, which is the size of a New York skyscraper, and reach the terrace to drop the gifts at my feet. Day one of the games ends at sundown. The sun is in descent.

Vor shakes water from his hair and presents me with a tablet-sized rock. The illustration on it draws my eye. He drops it at my feet, and I stand and thank him. "What is it?"

"A piece of land for you do with whatever you wish."

Damn. A piece of land of my own. I've never owned anything, not even a car. My palm itches to pick it up and take a closer look. There's a drawing and a written script I yearn to read. But I can't touch it. If I touch it, I've accepted it, and the games are over.

Although Dani secured Vor's win with me, Ark is competing in the games. I want to see his gift. I want to know what it is. I want to know he's alive. I want him to at least survive.

Sitting back down, I stare at the descending sun, not once paying attention to the stunned Dani, who's throwing eye daggers at me from the controls. I was supposed to accept Vor's gift right away. Granted, that was before Ark entered the games. She can't fault me for wanting to see his gift. After all, the prize (me) goes to the fittest predator, and Ark is definitely fit.

CHAPTER EIGHT

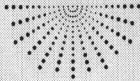

LENA

*T*he sun goes down.

Ark never shows.

I accept the parcel of land from Vor and announce that he's the winner.

My body cools, and inside, I feel hollow. I think Mae is sad. Or maybe I'm sad. But I better pussy up and smile and cheer because Dani's gonna kill me if she finds out I have feelings for her other son. If he's dead, and he probably is, I have to take care of myself and survive in the Ra court next to his cobra mother.

Most males cheer for Vor, and I mentally file the faces of the males who appear to be searching the crowds and whispering among one another. Even if I hadn't known bits and pieces of the Ra tribe's power struggles from living at Tash's place for a while, I would have figured it out on the second day I woke up in the palace.

After finding out I don't hunt for food, Dani invited me for breakfast. She served me a slab of raw meat and two uncooked eggs with a pretty dagger I could use to feed myself. I kept the dagger. It has jewels. I'm sure she noticed when I swiped it off the table and headed back to my quarters, but she said nothing about it, and so the dagger is now mine.

Sometimes I wish I had the balls to use it and cut her.

Right about now would be a good time as she glides toward me on the terrace and hugs me, kissing the spot on my earlobe she bit before.

"The eternal fires should burn brighter than ever now. Mae favors my son." She squeezes me tightly and whispers, "Does she not?"

"She favors your son." I say the truth, but commit to keeping secret what I believe is the whole truth and nothing but the truth. Ark is my favorite lie. Mae favors Dani's other son, the one who never returned, and since my chest feels hollow, I believe Mae is sad that Ark never presented her with a gift. Sad, however, is better than mad. Horror stories of Mae's wildfires burning villages and cities alike reached even my ears. Tribal scriptures, writings by Sha-males on the walls of the palace, convey that Mae is hot-tempered, as unpredictable and impulsive as fire. All she needs is a bit of gasoline, and she'll flare up and destroy everything in her path.

Some writings also say that Mae worked hand in hand with Aimea, goddess of doom, to destroy the predators altogether. I sure hope Mae's changed. I don't want to destroy anyone. Okay, well, maybe Dani, but that's neither here nor there now.

Vor approaches and kisses my lips, lingers there, and we lock eyes. I'm unsure what he sees in mine when he smiles fondly at me. "Mae will come around."

I wrap my arms around my body, rubbing my prickly, cold skin. "I'm gonna freeze out here." The shitty part about

Mae feeling sad? She doesn't burn inside me, so now I'm cold as fuck, my temperature likely that of a normal human, and I'm out here naked in below-zero temps.

"I need a coat," I say.

Vor shakes his head. "No, you need to return the fire to the pits."

I frown. "What do you mean?"

He takes me by my shoulders and spins me around. "Look up," he says.

The eternal flames that burn on the roof of a place called the Hall of the Eternal Flame are nothing but a flicker.

"What happened?" I ask.

"You tell me, human. Those flames have been burning since the dawn of our time. They don't go out. Ever."

"Maybe someone forgot to cut the wood and throw it up there." It happens. People forget shit.

Next to me, Dani sighs. "No, child, nobody forgot the wood. The flames burn because Mae's spirit burns bright atop her birthplace. Fire is the energy she left behind in the tribe. And if there's no fire or heat in the capital, people will freeze tonight."

"They shall freeze, then," I say. Stunned, I follow with "What?"

"What?" Vor repeats.

"I meant, we can all gather up wood and throw it up there. The Sha pray over it, and the fire burns. Done."

"You are a goddess of fire, are you not?" Dani bites out.

"Yeah, I think so."

"Or maybe the goddess has left you and you are nothing but prey, a meal I would devour in two spans, digest, and forget about."

"Mother," Vor bites out. "She is to be my Raiyes."

Dani narrows her eyes. "If she is to be a Raiyes, she will

need Mae's fire and all her lies. Ensure that the human understands she must embrace the goddess and control Mae's wily nature."

"Yes, Mother."

"Also, be sure she is bred tonight."

CHAPTER NINE

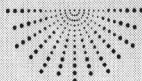

LENA

I've daydreamed about this night, wondering what my games would look like, who would compete, what kinds of wonderful gifts I would get, which male would win day one, and every time I pictured the night, I pictured spending it with Ark. He's won all the first nights I've witnessed him competing for, and so my daydreaming was realistic, or at least most expected.

That's not all, though.

Sometimes, I would venture into dreaming about his naked body on top of mine, grinding into me while chanting Mae's name. Flames would ignite on the ceiling, and all around us, the walls would burn as we burned with passion for each other.

I feel like a dumbass for even thinking about it. The reality is more like this: Dani sits on the throne, tapping her claws, glaring at the seven firepits the Sha-males are trying to light. At her feet, I'm shivering even though I'm well dressed and covered in furs. I had no idea how much these people depended on fire for heating in the winter until the fire died down. What's worse, before the winning couple retires for the night, it is customary to entertain the guests. And since this is a palace, there're thousands of guests gathered for the games, most of them earls and noble males of the Ra tribe.

To top it all off, if I'm not mistaken, another tribe Dani brought here, surely to seek alliance with once Vor is Rai, is in attendance. I think they gave Vor that piece of land for me. The writing on the tablet is not Ra. I can tell because I am also Mae, their mighty goddess, and my brain recognizes and reads their language.

Now, I'd really like to put my Mae-ness to use. Like, you know, start those seven fires and save my life from the cobra on the throne. If the fire won't burn, these people can't pray, and the poor Sha-males have gathered around the pit, nervously whispering and praying that the fire will ignite. While sparks pop here and there, nothing is catching. The herbs and flowers piled on top of the pits are starting to wilt, and Vor's snarling about the quality of the smoke. The smoke that he loves inhaling and that pretty much everyone in the land uses for meditation and jolly good times.

Dani's getting so mad, fire might come out of her ears.

Vor's pacing around the firepits, shouting at the Sha-males, making some of them cry.

I wish I could snap my fingers and make fire, but I can't.

Vor starts toward me. I gather up my fur as if it'll protect me. He crouches before me, eyes flashing the silver of his hunter, and he smiles just as Dani would smile, with one side of his mouth turned up.

"I have waited a long time for the perfect opportunity to take down my older brother, and I have done that now. I won the first night with the prize."

I nod. "Yes."

"It seems to me Mae is displeased."

"I wouldn't know anything about that."

He traces a claw over my cheek, down my jaw and lower, stopping at my pulse. If he slices, he'll bathe in my blood. I'm gonna die like a butchered pig. Who knows, maybe they'll turn me upside down and bleed me into the dead firepit.

"You are Mae, goddess of fire and lies. You will again be the Raiyes of your tribe. What more can I do for you?"

"I don't know, Vor. You have to believe me. I have no idea where Mae is or what she's doing."

Vor squeezes my throat, his eyes flashing silver now. "You want Ark? Is that it?"

I try shaking my head, but he's holding me too tightly.

Dani sits next to me. "Vor, my boy, we are in company."

"I don't care!" he shouts, and squeezes my throat tighter, pulling my face until it's inches from his.

"Ark is dead by now," Dani whispers. "Mae, you have your winner. Vor is the fittest predator, and he won fair and square."

Stars are playing over my eyes. I'm gonna pass out. "You're gonna...kill me," I choke out, and Vor releases my throat. I rub it and suck in desperate breaths, preparing to flee. Dani grabs my hand and won't let go. I try tugging, but can't.

They've trapped me. They want the fucking fire, and I can't give them fire. I don't know why the goddess is doing this, but she is, and I'm just a vessel for her shit.

"Tsk tsk tsk," comes from behind Vor. "Having a party and I'm not invited again?"

Vor spins and reveals Ark, who winks at him and takes a seat next to me, throwing an arm over my shoulders.

"Get your hands off her," Vor says.

"Or?" Ark chuckles. "You'll fight me?" He snorts.

"Welcome back, Ark," Dani says, her voice as pleasant as ever.

"I bet you're happy to see me."

"I thought you gave up when the effort to win proved too daunting," Dani says, retiring to the throne. She's like the overwatch, and Ark and I both have to turn on the steps below her to speak with her.

Ark laughs. "If I gave up, I wouldn't have the pleasure of negotiating with you, Mother."

Dani appears surprised. Her gaze sweeps the room and finds the tribemates attuned to their conversation. Ever so slightly, she tilts her head and rises from the throne. "Carry on," she says.

"With what?" a male asks.

Dani spins around. "Who asked that?"

A male with a dark brown beard hanging in a braid from his chin down to the middle of his chest steps out of the crowd. "There's no celebration. The goddess is displeased." He points. "Winter is here, and with no fire, Mae will freeze us all."

"Or worse," Ark says. "Burn the city to ashes."

"Or make us tell lies," another male says. "And quarrel with each other like you and yours."

"I can't do that," I say. "That's madness."

"Amti, Amti, Amti…" the Sha start chanting, and the crowds start murmuring. Amti is the goddess of madness and lust, which is how I feel most days.

Dani lifts her hands and says, "I will speak with Mae. She will return the fire, for she has picked her winner. All I ask for is some time. Celebrations will go on, as will the games."

Dani and Vor disappear behind what I always believed to be a wall, but now see is a portal into a room. I follow, then glance back at Ark, who gets up slowly and stretches before throwing an arm around my shoulders again. It's a proprietary gesture, and I try shaking him off, but he yanks a strand of my hair and says, "Stop fidgeting."

"Get your arm off me."

"No."

"What do you mean, no?"

"Is your translator malfunctioning?"

"No."

He smiles. "There, you said it."

I grip his wrist and wish for Mae to heat up my palm so I could burn him as a warning, but, of course, Mae isn't available when I need her, so together, Ark and I walk into the small dark sitting room with burgundy walls displaying drawings done with white chalk. At least it appears as if it's chalk. I don't have much time to marvel at the art, for Dani swings.

Ark grabs her wrist, then her throat. "I'm too old for slapping, Mother."

Vor steps in. "Release her."

Ark shakes Dani by her throat. "If anyone touches the human again, Mae might burn the city to ashes. Since I intend to rule over living predators and not ashes and bones, I can't let you harm the human." He releases Dani, and she moves closer to Vor, maybe seeking protection, maybe just making it appear as if she needs it.

"How did you survive?" she asks and, calmly as ever, walks to a service shelf. She runs her claw over several small bottles holding clear liquids. Picking out a vial, she shakes her head. "One of your spies must've entered the chambers and tampered with the poison. I shall find out who he is and burn him alive. Mae would like that, wouldn't you, Mae?"

"Sounds fun," I lie, because that's what she wants to hear and because I need to survive this fucking palace and live with this mother-in-law for the rest of my life. That sounds depressing. I smile anyway.

Dani mimics my smile. It looks awkward on her.

"No spies, Mother," Ark says, "Like I told you out on the terrace, it pays to be friends with our neighbors. Our wars

65

and the way we hunted them made them develop portals, medicine, and advanced ways of healing we never considered. Have you never wondered how the Ka survived all those turns against a much stronger opponent?"

"They survived because of your father's incompetence."

Ark snorts. "You mean your mate's incompetence?"

"You are right. Both my mates were a disappointment. That's why they're dead, and you shall join them."

"Maybe. Maybe not." Ark strokes my nape, and it's as if his thumb is brushing over my clit. I swear to God, any place he touches on my body feels like my clit.

"At the moment," Ark continues, "you have problems I can solve."

"We need fire," Vor says.

"Happy to hear your voice, brother."

"Shut up," Vor responds.

Ark sticks out his tongue, and for a second there, they remind me of how siblings are supposed to behave when twelve and arguing. It makes me think of my sister.

"I can give you fire," Ark says.

Dani giggles. "Has Mae possessed you too?"

Ark cracks his neck and adjusts his stance. He looks like he's gonna clonk her over the head. I'd like to whack her, but wouldn't dare. Eh, being prey truly blows.

Dani wears a familiar smirk. "Ark, my boy, if you think you can trick me into a deal like you've tricked that poor Nemrenian into your fold with promises of riches and lands, you would be wise to remember who raised you that way."

"I wouldn't dream of tricking you, Mother. I *can* give you fire."

She gives him a blank stare.

Ark blows her a kiss.

Dani rolls her eyes and sits on a log. "I'm listening."

Ark remains standing, his thumb still brushing the back

of my neck, and I hope they're all too busy to scent my arousal.

"Give me the human," Ark says, "and you'll have fire by the time the missing barrels of brew arrive."

"No," Vor says at the same time that Dani turns to Vor and asks, "We're out of brew?"

Vor grits his teeth. I think they might become blunt like mine if he continues grinding. A nod, and Dani turns to Ark. "How will you do it?"

"By giving Mae what she wants," Ark says.

"How do you know what she wants?" Dani asks.

"I smell it." He slaps my ass. I yelp and try to step away, but his arm is back over my shoulders, and he's gripping me in a way that makes it impossible to move. He's tucked me under his armpit. Spinning, Ark pulls up a portal and exits the room with me while I turn my head to see Vor seething behind us. He takes a step forward, but Dani puts her hand on his chest and whispers something in his ear. Her claws extend, and I know it can't be good for me.

"What happened in there?" I hiss at Ark.

"Dani traded away Vor's prize."

Oh my God. "You must know she did that for a reason and she thinks it's best for her."

"I know."

"Then why did you ask for me?" When he doesn't answer, I look up and prompt him again. "Why did you do it?"

Ark keeps walking as if I'm not speaking to him.

Ark will take me for the night, but I doubt anyone besides the family circle will realize Vor traded away his prize.

As we walk the hallways that lead back to my room, Ark releases me, content to march in front of me and whistle while I stew on this: the goddess is the only thing the predators want. Without her, I'm food. If Ark knows a way to get the fire going tonight, I'm in.

CHAPTER TEN

ARK

I march into Mae's chambers feeling the same way I felt when I marched into Hart's chambers on day three of the Ka tribal games to claim my prize, the female who is now his marked mate, Amti, goddess of madness and lust. Like a winner, my chest is full of success and pride. I stole Mae right from under Vor's nose.

The door slams behind me, and I smell that the prey is in the chambers and not outside. Another win. She didn't run. Granted, I'd have caught her before she took three steps, so no pleasure in the chase, but it would be nice to tackle her in the hallway and make her pussy bleed before we got to the furs in this opulent chamber.

I'm standing in the sitting space across from the painting of Bera, goddess of fertility and war. She's sitting on furs and nursing a baby from one of her fine tits. Her mouth is covered in blood. An itch develops in my left ball, and I scratch it. Another itch on my calf. I scratch that too. My skin starts crawling, and I wanna scratch my entire body. Fucking goddesses and their powers. I can sense them. We all can. It's utterly uncomfortable.

"Mae?" I say into the dark room. "You will need firelight to see."

Torches ignite, illuminating the room in a seductive low light. I doubt Mae lit up the palace fires as well, but this is a start and tells me my instincts were right about this. Some of the discomfort in my body wanes, and I sigh, relieved that Mae's content again.

The stab wounds that I can't heal because of the poison still running in my blood hurt. I start undressing, remove the three belts covering the wounds so I didn't bleed all over my mother. I can't give her that much satisfaction. I prefer to keep her guessing.

Thinking about my mother makes me smile. Fondly. She's in the chambers with Vor, screaming and yelling at him right now. I'll find out what she said later.

Sha-males have ears and eyes everywhere in the palace. They're not supposed to speak of what they hear from the ruling parties, but this Sha is the exception to the rule. He's my sister's male, and the one she castrated as a sacrifice to Bera. I'd kill anyone with a dagger aimed at my balls, but for the Sha, it's an honor that Bera accepted his detached package.

Blood trickles down my hip. I swipe the trail with my thumb and taste for poison. Still there. I spit and wipe my mouth.

It is what it is. No antidote. No cure. I'm gonna die. The good part is that I'm not gonna die tonight.

Before removing my ierto, I glance at Mae. She's standing by the door, arms crossed under her tits. Her nipples are small and perky and standing up, hard already. I see it through the soft, thin leather she's wearing over her tits. I'm gonna have those tits in my mouth here in a few moments.

"What are you looking at?" I ask and unsnap my ierto, flexing my cock.

She's keeping her pretty green eyes locked with mine. My hunter wants to tear her up for not lowering her gaze as prey should. But then I remember that the human is also a goddess, and Mae wouldn't lower her gaze to any predator, not even the fittest one.

"Nothing," she answers.

I snort. "It's not nothing, and you're welcome to look."

"Get over yourself, Ark."

I remove my boots and, with a wince, sit by the pool to dip my legs in to the knees. I groan as I lean back to rest on my palms. My cock is half erect, resting on my thigh.

Clothed humans don't make me horny as much as naked ones, and this naked human makes me want to shove my dick down her throat and make her choke on it. "Join me," I say.

She shakes her head.

"You can't stand there all night."

"I can," she says.

"But you won't. Join me."

She shakes her head again.

"I need you to sew the wounds back together."

She frowns. "Why aren't they healing?"

"They'll heal when you sew the skin." I motion her over. "Come."

She hesitates. "You didn't need to undress for me to do that."

"I didn't. But you like admiring my fitness. It turns you on."

"Does not." Pretty red cheeks show the human is lying. Mae hasn't quite gotten hold of Lena yet. If she had, the human wouldn't show visual cues of her lies.

I'm unaccustomed to defiance, and her resistance to sit with me irritates me and pleases me at the same time. I'm pleased she doesn't fear me or the consequences of her disobedience. I reach into my ierto, and the pain saps my breath. I cough and cringe at my weakness while rummaging through the pockets. Where the fuck is the sewing kit the Ka gave me before I left?

After Vor stabbed me and left me for dead, I *portaled* into the chambers of Hart, the leader of the Ka tribe with whom I have an uneasy alliance until I can secure the throne and pass laws that will punish those who incite wars and reward those who make the lands thrive. We've warred enough, so much and for so long that we have risked our survival. Only the fittest can survive, and in order to be fit, one must reproduce. Well, in the wars, our females stopped being fertile, and theirs are all dead.

If we continued with the wars, Aimea, the goddess of doom would come. We couldn't allow that, so Hart and I made peace.

That's why he helped me patch up the wounds, but even he can't give me the antidote.

Mae kneels beside me and rests a small clawless hand atop mine. "What are you looking for?" she asks, green eyes blinking, the eyelashes extended and colored pitch black. The sun spots on her nose wrinkle, and she makes a face as if she smells something bad.

I sniff my armpit and almost faint. Yeah, better get bathing now. I wouldn't come near me either.

"Ark," she says.

My dick jumps. "Yeah?"

"What are you looking for?"

I frown, temporarily forgetting what I was doing. Her beauty tends to have that effect on me. I'm surprised I remember my name. Good thing my dick remembered and woke up when she called me.

"Wound sewing kit."

Mae digs into my pockets and takes out stones, twigs, and

a needle as large as her finger. When she leans in some more, her breasts almost spill out of the loose confinement she wears tonight. She pulls out a leather thread. "This it?"

It takes a gigantic effort for me to look from her breasts to her face. She's holding up the needle and thread Hart gave me. They're supposed to reinforce the closure of wounds in case we're struck with poison-laced daggers. It's perfect for treating the open wounds and forcing them to close, but the poison inside my body will stay.

I must be staring at her blankly, because Mae repeats the question, to which I just nod like a love bug who found his buggette.

I lift my arm and fist it. With my other arm, I grip the edge of the pool, my jaw tight. "Make it quick."

Mae kneels next to me and prepares to close the wound that ripped open, the one Vor gave me. The other wounds the Ka took care of, though I have no idea if the skin over them will self-heal. Guess we'll see, won't we?

First, Mae cleans the dagger jab with a cloth, which in itself hurts more than that one time Tash kicked me in the balls for pushing him into a hole in the ground and camping above it for the night. At the time, it was funny. I was twelve and wanted to know if my big brother could get out of a prison hole on his own. Of course, he could. My big brother is my hero. He waited until I fell asleep above, climbed up, and kicked me in the balls. I remember the pain exploding in my belly.

This pain is exploding in my lungs now, and I want to curl up and whine in hunter, but can't because hunters scare humans. Besides, as soon as the wound is closed and I'm bathed, I'll be bleeding Mae's little pussy. The vision of her wriggling under me eases the torture of her little fingers pushing the needle through my skin.

"This is gross. Gross. Gross," she whispers and bends over to vomit in my bath.

I stare at her.

She wipes her mouth. "Sorry."

"We'll use the other bath."

Nodding, she finishes closing my wound, and I resist squealing like a terrik as I rise, my dick rising along with me, expanding, broadening, reaching midway up my belly.

Instead of admiring my fitness, Mae focuses on the image of Bera holding a wee baby.

I point. "That's you as a baby."

The human busies herself with cleaning the needle and thread. Since she vomited in this pool, I'll use the pool near the bedroom. Even better. "Leave it and come with me." I open the portal that leads to the bedroom and leave the sitting room.

Mae's chambers are like the heavens. The strong scent of prey in her habitat makes my mouth water, and I inhale a lungful, then cough, holding my sides, hoping I don't rip open the damn stitches.

"Nah," the female says and stops next to me. "That's Mae. My mother got rid of me the second I popped out of her womb." The human stands there expecting me to respond, and so I do.

"Your father raised you well." Since females roam from male to male, mothers leaving their babies is natural in the tribes.

She shrugs. "Don't know who that man is."

She's an abandoned pup. That must've been tough. I take her hand and this time intertwine our fingers. "For what it's worth, sometimes it's best not to know who your parents really are."

"You think so?"

"I know so." The room is covered in darkness, and I wonder if the human will try to walk around blindly or actually light the torches. I leave her to decide and walk us through Mae's bedroom, a simple place with a massive bed and a small pool of rejuvenating water. The minerals found in this water won't heal my wounds, but they relieve muscle soreness and thereby build agility, which I'll need tomorrow as the poison keeps spreading through my body, making me weaker than I normally am.

Unfit.

Of all the fucking spans! I snarl.

The human jerks her hand away.

"Excuse me," I say. "I'm thinking."

"Violent thoughts?"

"Always." I chuckle.

I place her before the foot of the bed and tell her to sit, which she does. There. Some obedience. Pleased, I dip into the pool and sigh. Resting my head against the pool's edge, I relax my tired body.

"Is firelight the only way predators see at night?"

"We see in the dark."

"Of course you do. I knew that, but I'm just wondering if firelight is the only way for me to see."

"There's other ways."

"Now would be a good time to tell me those ways."

"Bugs," I tell her and lift my head. Mae's removing the fur choker my mother must've given her. It's Ka fighter fur. Very old, from back when my grandfather hunted.

"Bugs?" she asks.

"Mmhm. There're bugs that like dark places and light up during mating and pregnancy, which is all the time, pretty much. They appear like tiny stars."

"And how are they used for light?"

"They stick to walls and live there."

Looking around, Mae bites her lip. "There're no bugs here, right?"

"Nah."

She scratches her arm. "You sure?"

"Do you fear bugs?"

"No."

I narrow my eyes. "A lie."

"I hate bugs. They creep me out. I like creepy things, don't get me wrong, but not bugs. They crawl. You understand?"

"You fear bugs," I conclude. "Are bugs predators on earth?"

"Um, some are I guess. Like spiders."

"What is their size?" I'm trying to gauge this predator's fitness.

Mae makes a circle by connecting her thumb with another finger. "Like, this big, usually, but some are as big as my fist."

What the fuck? "I expected a larger creature."

Mae shakes her head. "Sometimes small creatures are more dangerous. See, some spiders are poisonous and they sting. You die. The end."

"How appropriate."

Mae tilts her head. "What do you mean?"

"Never mind."

Mae falls silent, hangs her head, folds her hands in her lap. I don't remember the human being quiet and demure at Tash's. Something is bothering her. I tap my claw on the pool's edge. "What's the matter with you, human?"

She snaps her head my way. "Oh, let's see. For one, I can't see in a dark room. For two, I don't know how to set shit on fire when everyone tells me I'm the goddess of fire."

I lean in for more, but nothing comes. "Is there no three?"

"You're an asshole."

I rise out of the water, watching Mae's alarmed face. She

can see my eyes glowing in the dark. Before her, I crouch. "You are my prize."

"I know."

"Then you know you will bleed tonight."

"You wouldn't dare hurt me, predator," Mae says. I can almost feel the goddess's presence in the way the human speaks, in the way her eyes almost light up with a fire of their own.

"I heard rumors," I say and peck her mouth, then trail my nose down her cheek and neck all the way to her shoulder. I bite the seam of the flimsy cloth and rip it, tearing off the sleeve. Her heart beats faster. The prey is...scared. The scent of her fear excites me, making me hungry. Wanting to fuck my prey is more complicated than I expected.

"What rumors?" she asks.

I rip the other sleeve. "That human pussy bleeds the first time it's penetrated. I've been looking forward to it since I heard about it."

"Oh, I see." She clears her throat. "That's how you want to make me bleed."

"Mmhm." I kiss her neck and she shudders with bumps rising on her skin. She parts her legs, and I pull the leather string holding her corset together. The top collapses into her lap, spilling out her breasts.

I kiss up her neck and reach her mouth, coaxing it to open with my tongue. The second our tongues connect, I growl at the taste of her. A prey creature and a goddess all wrapped into a single taste that can only be described as divine. I grab the back of her head and kiss her as if I'll devour her. Toppling her onto the bed, I rip her skirt.

She's holding the back of my head and pulling me to her as if wanting to eat my face. Her legs lock around my waist, and my cock just about penetrates the pussy I want to enjoy. It takes a huge effort to peel my mouth from hers, and when

I do, she yanks my hair and pulls me back, then sticks her tongue into my mouth.

I kiss her again while taking her wrists into one hand and holding them, then rise on my knees so I can view my pretty prey. She's sprawled before me, tattered dress around her, her beautiful curves on display. "You're even prettier up close."

Mae chuckles. "I know you've stalked the baths over at your brother's house."

I nod, though she can't see that I have. Bending, I kiss the side of her breast. Mae tries to move her hands, but I've got them. I squeeze her wrists tighter as I shift to her nipple and lick. She gasps, and I suck on the pale smooth goodness as if it's gonna give me the antidote I need.

I move to the next one, my cock painfully aroused, leaking fluid on her thigh. I hear it dripping on her skin. Swiping some of it, I smear it on her mouth.

Mae licks the seed.

I kiss her, locking my eyes with her green ones. "Let's make fire."

CHAPTER ELEVEN

LENA

*L*et's make fire.

Ark stretches over my body, his firm muscles pressing against my softness, making the butterflies in my belly unfurl and, lower yet, my pussy throb. I angle my head so he can kiss my neck all he likes. I even lift my hips and rub all over his long hard length. I've never imagined a dick could be this big.

If fitness is measured in cock inches, Ark's the winner. *Tash comes in pretty close.* I don't know where that thought came from, and I swallow, feeling awkward about Ark's brother's dick coming into my brain right now.

Ark lifts a bit. I can't see what he's doing, but I'm fairly certain he propped himself on his elbows.

"What is it?" he asks.

Jesus. How can he tell I'm all twisted in the head? It's not that I'm thinking of his brother, it's just that I saw Tash nude once and it was greatly unexpected and shocking as fuck to see his penis freely leaking semen. Also, massive-cock effect is real. Makes a girl stare at it and remember it for the rest of her life.

"You said we should make fire," I evade. Goddess of lies to the rescue. I wonder if he'll buy it and we can forget about my temporary insanity that ruined our moment. I'm pretty sure we could've fucked by now.

What the hell is wrong with me? I'll remain a virgin even after a night with Ark. Must be a record of some sort. Lord, I need to stop thinking. He needs to start talking. "Ark?"

"Something happened. What was it?"

"I was thinking," I say.

"Violent thoughts?"

"Um, no, but they might make you violent."

"I like it. Tell me."

Tell him, a voice whispers in my head. Totally unwise. There's no way I'd tell.

"Don't make me repeat myself and don't lie, Mae."

"I was comparing two cocks."

"What?"

"Your cock and the other cock I saw."

"You mean my brother's?"

"Is that weird?"

"No. My brother has a mighty cock. If you weren't impressed, I'd think something was wrong with either you or his cock."

"You're not mad?"

"No, baby. You're under me, and a night with me will erase the memory of anything else."

Typical Ark. He thinks so highly of what he can do in the sheets that nobody is a threat to his bedroom prowess.

"I wish I was that confident," I tell him.

"It comes with practice," he whispers. "Don't worry, Mae. You will make fire."

"I wish I could."

"You can and you will."

I run a hand over his big braid. It's coarse and long, his

hair shaved at the sides of his head and tightly twisted at the top into one large braid that he decorates with leather strings and beads. As I thumb one bead, he starts purring, then lowers his head to my breasts, first the left, then the right. His rough tongue makes my nipples perk up. It's both ticklish and arousing, and I moan, wriggling under him.

Ark purrs louder as he positions his head between my legs. He grips my legs under my knees and yanks me down the bed so that my ass hangs over the edge. I look down, and all I see are the silver eyes of his hunter lowering, and then I feel the first lick. It nearly sends me off the bed. "Oh my God."

A tiny flame flickers on the torch affixed to the wall above the bed.

Ark chuckles and licks my pussy again, this time swiping with his entire tongue. It's a big tongue, and it swipes my wet slit back and forth. My pussy pulses, and I arch my back, my eyes rolling as I stare at the wall behind me, where the torches burn again. Ark spreads my pussy with his thumbs and licks inside while his finger strokes my small hole.

My body ignites, heat rushes into my fingers, and I pant as he licks and strokes me, even putting my legs over his shoulders so I'm straddling his face. I lock my ankles and fist his hair, pushing down his face and running my pussy over it so I can get traction on my clit.

Ark catches on pretty quickly and sucks my clit into his mouth, then flicks it with that wicked big tongue.

"Oh no," I whisper. The fire burns over the ceiling as if it's a living thing, and my hands in his hair light up. "The ceiling is on fire," I say, and pant because he's gonna make me come and I think I might burn the house down.

Ark's mumbling something incoherent. I lift onto my elbows. His eyes are closed as he eats my pussy and thumbs my back hole, not entering, only teasing. It's like he's making love to my pussy. It's sexy, and I smile just as he snaps open his eyes.

All silver of his hunter.

He purrs loudly and licks me while we watch each other and while heat churns in my belly. I grip the sheets with one hand, the other fisting his hair, and I hold on for the orgasm that's coming. Ark sucks on my clit and twists his mouth, and I scream my release.

The fire spreads over the walls, and I'm still coming, aftershocks making my pussy spasm, leak more cum.

Ark's lapping up the cum, and he's purring his lungs out as if it's something that tastes amazing to him. Once done, he climbs over me and sticks his tongue into my mouth.

I taste myself.

He takes my hands and throws them over his shoulders. I hug him tightly and watch the inferno on the ceiling until Ark traps my cheeks between his palms and forces me to look into the eyes of his hunter. They're silver and clear, and I like them better than the white eyes because his silver is more expressive.

"Even your eyes are wild," he says.

"What do you mean?" I ask, then hitch a breath as he settles between my legs, his cock poised at my wet entrance. If he jerks his hips, he'll penetrate me, but he doesn't. Although I'm trapped under him, he won't push in, and my pussy is throbbing. I lift my hips, but he growls a warning.

"I don't like to be teased, predator," comes out of my mouth, my voice sounding like a musical instrument, a violin. It's eerily similar to the way Imani spoke when Bera got hold of her.

"Mae," Ark says. "I wondered when you'd come to me."

The flames settle down, and the fire burns quietly as if listening to us. Ark looks around, then back down at me. "You've picked the prettiest human to inhabit."

"Thank you." Heat crawls up my cheeks, and I'm sure I'm blushing.

Ark repositions his body, his cock back at my opening. I suck in a breath and hold it, preparing for pain.

The tip of him enters, and I watch his eyes hood and listen to the pleasant alluring purr from his chest that vibrates on my breasts.

"Breathe out slowly," he says, voice laced with his purr. It's both sexy and comforting.

I do as I'm told as he pushes more of his length into me, now closing his eyes and breathing out himself. He grabs my butt cheek and stretches me more so he can penetrate deeper. Pain makes my eyes water, and tears slip out from the corners.

He licks them, purring even louder and pushing inside me more.

I claw at his back, bite his bottom lip, and stiffen as he pulls back and slowly pushes inside, this time more easily than before. He does this several times, pulling out and pushing into me, and the pain subsides, and the heat in my belly returns with each of his strokes, and I stop clawing at his back and hug him closely and stare at the ceiling, feeling the fires rage on the roof.

It simply hovers in the sky and burns, and I know for a fact I am capable of things my brain can't conceive of, and because I can't conceive of it, I can't believe it. I can't control it. What if I started believing in myself?

Ark nuzzles my neck and begins growling. He props his hands on the bed and moves his hips at a fast pace. I rest my palms on his chest and feel his muscles flex under them. I stroke his torso, admiring his fitness, my pussy getting wetter and wetter, easing the path of his cock in and out of me.

When my eyes return to his face, Ark's eyes are closed,

and I am free to watch him get lost in the pleasure. I want to stay like this with him forever.

That's not possible, so I savor this moment in time and close my eyes as well. I grab hold of his biceps so I can feel them flex under my palms.

Together, we come.

CHAPTER TWELVE

ARK

The green of her eyes transfixes me. I could stare at them for the rest of my life, which is precisely what I'll be doing for this night or next night before I die. Unless I can get the antidote from wherever my mother placed it, presumably inside her chambers. Which are heavily guarded.

Which I haven't approached since I was a boy.

And I can't approach now, not even with hidden portals, because Mother is better guarded than Amti inside Hart's bedroom, and that's saying something because Hart's a paranoid motherfucker.

The human bites her lip again. I want to bite it for her, but can't for fear I'll break the skin and taste her blood and like it. I turn on my side, and my still-erect cock leaves her holy pussy. Streaks of her human virgin blood are painted on my dick and mixed in with my semen. My dick is looking prettier than any of Bera's paintings.

With a thumb, I swipe some blood and taste it.

"Gross," the human says.

"Mmmmm." The blood is sweet, like nectar from a

goddess's tit. Not that I ever tasted that, but it's a saying when something is this yummy. "You taste better than terrik, human."

"That's really disturbing."

I wink and grab her, tuck her closer, and kiss her on the nose. "Are you tired?"

"Not yet."

Hmm, it was a yes-or-no question I asked deliberately because human females confuse me. *Not yet* I will translate as a no. "Hungry?" I add.

She purses her lips and looks up as if she has to think about it. What's there to think about? By Herea, humans are strange.

"Not much," she says.

Another *no*. I'll hunt her something in the morning.

"My name is Lena," she says. "In case you're wondering."

"I'm not wondering."

"Just saying since you keep calling me human or Mae."

I chuckle. "I'll call you whatever I please, and there's nothing you can do about it."

"Just want to be sure you know my name in case you want to use it. Or in case I stop responding when you don't use it."

I peck her shoulder and tuck her under me again, then penetrate her. "Lena," I whisper in her ear and pull out, then push back in. Her pussy wraps around my cock and holds it for dear life. It looks pretty, pink, and tastes like Bera's nectar. "I'll call you anything I want."

The human is hitching breaths, and her hooded eyes are closing.

I pick up my pace, fuck her harder, grip her neck, and purr at her ear. "Lena," I say, and the human's pussy spasms. "Your name on my lips is the magic word, hm?"

She grabs fistfuls of my hair, and my hunter claws at my

skin, so I growl and nip her shoulder. Lena yelps the way prey often does, and I want to fuck and devour her at the same time. Growling at her neck, I watch her pulse and lick it as if I'm prepping the prey for consumption. She grabs my head and forces my ear to her lips. "Ark," she says in a voice that makes me shudder, "I am your prey to pleasure or to hurt. Which will you choose?"

I almost bite the human. Fuck, coupling with a human is harder than I anticipated. I need to deal with the instincts. How is Tash dealing with the instincts? To eat and to fuck. They're both primal. And I want to know how to make this easier. I don't have time to learn how to be with her. I'm gonna die tomorrow or, hell, I even might not wake up in the morning.

Freezing on top of her, I pause. Considering I have only a short time left, it occurs to me that I chose to spend that time with her.

That ought to tell me something. What's my instinct trying to tell me? I should be with my brother Tash, drinking, smoking, talking about nothing and everything, maybe even sharing silence.

But I'm not.

I'm here, wrapped in the scent of prey and firelight. "I choose pleasure."

CHAPTER THIRTEEN

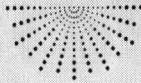

LENA

*A*rk and I fucked until I couldn't bear his cock anymore. Sitting up, I note wetness on my belly and wipe it away with my hand before looking down. Blood stains my palm. It's his blood. I glance at Ark, and sure enough, he's watching me. I feel like he's always watching me. It's a bit intense. I wish he'd tire and sleep so I could watch him instead.

"Tell me why you're still bleeding." Something isn't right.

"No."

Typical Ark. I shake my head. "Why aren't you changing into your hunter form so you can heal faster?"

"It's not a form. It is who I am."

I roll my eyes and make my way to the water. Dipping into the bath, I wince at the soreness between my legs. Hallelujah, my pussy is sore and I'm not a virgin anymore. There should be champagne and fireworks, though I did blow out the roof and set the sky on fire. That's pretty celebratory in this neck of the woods.

I lean my elbows on the bath's edge.

Ark lies on his side, props up his head with his arm, and scratches his balls. It's such a dude thing, I want to laugh, but I don't because I want to know why he's not healing. Predators self-heal. The wound I stitched up is still bleeding. This means the skin isn't sealing like it should.

"You know what I mean when I say hunter form."

"Knowing what you mean and you being correct in your meaning aren't the same. I am a hunter."

"Why aren't you in hunter now?" I press him again.

"Because your pussy wasn't gonna bleed itself, and the hunter can't make it bleed."

"But we're done with the bleeding pussy now, so…"

He strokes his hard cock. "We're not done."

"I'm sore," I whine.

"So?" He winks.

I chuckle. "No pain, no gain, huh?"

He smiles. "That is well said."

"I'm taking credit for it."

Ark laughs. He's relaxed now, less imposing, less of an asshole. His guard is down, and being alone with him now reminds me of being alone with him at Tash's. When we're alone, he's different, but it's not just that. He gives me all his attention and makes me feel like I'm the only person in the world. Nobody's ever made me feel that way, and I love him for it. I do. Sad but true, and typical of a teenager. Falling for the asshole.

"One of the stitches gave out," he says.

"Oh, so it's the stitching problem, not a healing problem?" I tease.

"Mmhm. Come back to bed and see for yourself."

I climb onto the bed and start feeling awkward and more than a little embarrassed over what happened between us. I'm trying to be all adult and cool about it, but I did lose my virginity a few hours ago to a male of another species, who is also a predator, an animal, really.

On the bed, I sit next to Ark, one knee up and my cheek resting on it, facing him. The wound seeps blood. "I can patch that up."

"It'll do fine till morning."

"What are you planning to do in the morning?" I presume he has a game plan for day two. It would be nice if he shared the plan with me. Perhaps I could help. Perhaps Mae could, even if we're not in tune with each other.

"Things," he says and picks up my finger, flicking the blunt fingernail with a claw. "Don't worry about what I gotta do." Ark drops my finger, his gaze on the fire in the pit. The silence of the four-foot flame in the firepit is unfamiliar but comforting. Usually when fire burns, it's accompanied by the crackling of the twigs and wood falling or shifting in the pit. In complete violation of the laws of nature, this fire burns out of nothing. "My family's business is not your problem."

"We're going on day two in the games tomorrow." My heart starts pounding. I'm excited and nervous as fuck. Vor won't give me up this easily. He likes me. I can tell. He likes me, but he's also unstable. And even if he didn't like me, he wouldn't give up the Ra throne. Whoever wins the goddess gets the throne. That's what Dani said, and Dani is well versed in power plays. As far as everyone knows, Vor won day one.

"You always win day one," I comment, again trying to get him to speak about the wound. "Was this your first loss?"

"I still won you."

"You won a night with me."

"No, I won you."

I shake my head. He's impossible. And right, but I'm not gonna tell him that. "What were you going to gift me?"

Ark stands and pauses to shake his head before walking to his ierto and taking something out. He returns with a pair of white fur gloves. He throws them on the bed and lies back down with a barely audible whine. I know he's in pain. He won't admit it, though. Fitness is everything for these guys.

I pick up the gloves and rub them on my cheek. "They feel so good."

"They're for your hands, not the face."

"I know. I'm just rubbing them on my face."

"Why?"

"Because..." I shrug. "The fur feels like something I'd want to rub on my face. It's nice."

"I have a whole hunter of fur. Wanna rub it and feel nice?"

"Yes! Yes, I would. If you hunter up, I'll cuddle next to it and sleep in its fur."

Ark's eyes narrow. "Are you trying to get me to heal?" On all fours, he crawls on top of me.

I press a palm over his chest, feeling the firm muscles. I love how fit he is.

"Maybe. If I asked for a hunter, would you bring him forth?"

Bones crack, and Ark's face starts contorting. His elbow blows out, and an arm starts thickening and extending, his hand becoming a paw. His claws flex, and my gaze travels from the paw to his face.

"Oh God," I whisper and start trembling. Ark in hunter is over seven feet tall, with gray-white fur, a massive head, huge ears that stand up, a bulky frame, and teeth that are all huge canines and sharp like daggers. The upper lip doesn't fold over the mouth, so the entire set of teeth is exposed.

Silver eyes stare down at me.

Saliva drips on my cheek. I'm terrified and regret asking him to do this.

The animal leans down to sniff me. He lingers and keeps

sniffing my face and neck, and I wonder when he's gonna bite down and kill me. But he hops off the bed and lies down in the corner of the room.

I grab the furs and join him on the floor, watching the fire dance around the room.

CHAPTER FOURTEEN

LENA

*H*alf-awake, I get a creepy feeling someone is watching me. Slowly, I blink open my eyes and turn my head. Ark stands next to the furs wearing a black ierto with bits and pieces of fur hanging from hooks at the bottom of it. No wait. Those are tails, ears, claws, even a paw that's decorating his ierto. Rubbing my eyes, I groan out, "Good morning."

"Rise, goddess. You're late for the games."

"Late?" I leap out of bed, panicked. Dani hates lateness, thinks it's a sign of degenerative behavior that grows worse as the person gets older, meaning when I turn thirty, I'll never go anywhere and do anything and waste away in bed. I grab the leaves I chew in the morning in lieu of brushing teeth and spit them out, then rinse.

Ark makes a disgusted face.

I chuckle. "It's just a little green leaf. Here, try one."

Ark shakes his head. Predators are carnivores.

I almost jog to the sitting space where the servants Dani assigned to me leave the clothes and find nothing. "Fuck. No dress."

"My mother," Ark says from behind me, "won't sacrifice any more of her dresses to Mae."

"I need clothes. It's freezing out there." I'm not cold, but I hear the winds whoosh outside. They're whipping against the palace walls.

"Mae seldom wore clothes. In winter, when the world is frozen, Mae walked over icy roads. Under her foot, everything melted. It was a show of her power." Ark hands me one of his belts. "Dress me instead."

Grabbing a heavy belt, I circle it around his body, fastening the belt in the front, and at the same time giving myself permission to smell him. I don't know why I find his scent sexy, but I do. It's petrichor, the scent of forest after rain, and although the forest is an earthy kind of scent, his is not a calming one, but more sexy, aggressive, dirty. I press my nose to his chest and inhale, then step away, my head up, eyes wide. "Fuck, I'm smelling you like a dog."

He stares down at me. "What is a dog?"

"A furry domestic animal that humans keep as pets."

Ark shows me his teeth and his eyes crinkle at the corners. "Appropriate, pet."

I narrow my eyes. "Very funny. Got more belts?"

Nodding, he gets another. As I fasten the second black belt above his ierto, I stop at the stab wound right under his rib cage. Although it's sealed, the skin around the wound has turned an indigo color. "Does this look right to you?"

Ark hesitates. "Yes," he finally answers me.

A lie, rings in my head in a voice that's not mine and in a language I shouldn't understand. "Oh my God," I whisper at Ark. "I've got Mae in the head."

Ark scratches his belly, back, and shoulder then steps away. "What did she say?"

"She says you're lying."

Ark scratches his nose and takes another step back.

I follow him. "Are you lying?"

He props his hands on his hips and juts his chin out, then nods.

I swallow. "What's wrong with you? And don't lie, I'll know." I press a finger to my temple. "She'll tell me."

"It is not a she. She is you as much as my hunter is me."

"Got it. I'll work on that. What's wrong with you?"

"The night before the games started, I got stabbed with a poisoned dagger."

I press a hand over my mouth. "Oh no. Wha... Wha..." Tears cloud my eyes.

Ark snarls. "Don't fucking pity me, Mae."

"I'm sorry."

Ark stomps to the window. "Stop crying for me."

"How can I not? You're telling me your mother poisoned you."

"I didn't say my mother poisoned me."

I frown. He's right. He never said that. How do I know this? "She did. I'm sure of it, but I don't know how I know."

"Mae knows."

"How?"

"She knows what orda-poisoned wounds look like."

"That doesn't explain why I accused your mother."

Ark chuckles. "Like knows like."

I approach the side window and glance at Dani standing on the terrace. Feli is chatting with Vor, who's flipping a dagger between his fingers. I wonder if that was the dagger he stabbed Ark with. Nah. Vor couldn't stab Ark even if he wanted to. Ark's fitter. He's the fittest of the Ra predators, but also a real asshole. "If you're trying to offend me, you've succeeded. I'm nothing like your mother."

"You're worse."

"Excuse me?" I spin around to face him.

"And now that you smell like prey, irresistible." He lowers

his head as if to peck my cheek, but I step back, fisting my hands. The fire burning above us in the sky flares. Mae is getting pissy. Maybe she'll burn off Ark's hair.

Unfazed, Ark grabs another belt and starts to fasten it around his body. He keeps dropping the belt and snarling at it until he finally throws it away. The poison weakens him, which will serve Vor in the games. Ark's ripe for the picking.

"Dani has chosen my winner for me," I conclude. I've always known this. It's just that Ark never fit into the games. After I ended up in Ralna, I didn't think he'd show up to compete for me.

He nods. "But you are a goddess, and you chose me." Ark points at his chest. "Mae chose me."

"But *I* haven't chosen anyone," I say.

"Mae has chosen already."

"But I haven't," I repeat.

"You have two spans and a night left."

"I might spend it with Vor."

Ark's on me in a second, arms wrapped around me. He kisses the top of my head. "Not if you play the game right."

I want him to say my name over and over again. It's important I preserve myself because Mae's power tempts me to get lost in her lies. It's almost madness, really, having the spirit of a goddess speaking in my head. "Say the magic word again."

He puts me at arm's length and winks. "Pussy."

He throws a small dark ball that pops open a portal, and disappears, leaving me to the vipers. Just as well. I can't be seen walking out of my quarters with him when, for all anyone knows, Vor won last night with me.

Opening the door to the terrace, I step outside into the bitter cold winds and the falling snow.

Under my feet, the ice accumulated on the terrace starts to melt.

CHAPTER FIFTEEN

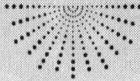

ARK

When Mother poisoned me, she ensured both Vor's victory and her reign over the Ra tribe. All he had to do was get rid of me on span one, and he couldn't even execute that simple task. Simple because at the moment, I'm not hard to kill. Snorting, I rub my side on the tree and scratch my wound.

In hunter, the wound itches even more as it's healing. The wound will heal, but the poison is still gonna run its course. I have no idea who (other than my mother) might have the antidote or even if there is one. My mother learned botany from Ra's finest Sha-male, who suddenly died in his sleep.

The male died right before the vote for the Ra throne took place, and everyone knew this high-ranking Sha was going to vote against my stepfather and designate himself as the temporary leader until Tash could ascend to the throne. Tash never made it to the throne. Mother put my stepfather and Vor's father on the throne because that's who she could control.

Tash and I were already labeled as outlaws, and she made

sure she alienated us. We were just too young and too stupid to see it back then.

Tash's scent surrounds me now that I've portaled to his earldom. I scratch myself on another tree, leaving my bleeding wound scent all over it. In hunter, I stop and sniff the blood, then sneeze.

Smells bad. Lemme lick it.

Mmm. Still smells bad.

Oh hey, a bug.

I snap my teeth and catch it in my mouth. It buzzes for a moment longer before I crush it with my back teeth. Sweet bug guts spill into my mouth, and I lap them up with my tongue. Much better tasting than my wound, and I hope I don't have to lick my body to clean it, because I might throw up.

Soft footsteps sound behind me. I raise my nose and sniff. Tash.

Spinning around, I whip my tail. Leaves fly around me, and one lands on my nose. I huff out a breath and Tash snorts, laughter in hunter. He's carrying a dead terrik between his teeth. It's probably for Bera, and it'll probably end up cooked, which I find a waste of a fine kill. I haven't eaten, and hunting while wounded is difficult.

In hunter, I eye his meal.

Tash stops and lowers his head, growling at me.

I growl back. I'm hungry, and I want his kill.

Leaning backward, I prepare to jump and take it from him.

"Predator," calls a voice that carries through the forest on the wind.

Tash's ears twitch, so I know he heard it, and I sure as fuck heard it. With my back leg, instead of jumping, I scratch my belly, behind my ears, rub my face into the dirt. Fucking hate having goddesses around. Love it too. It's confusing.

Tash drops the terrik and leans back. His leg bones disjoin and pop out of the sockets while his neck shrinks and his trunk widens and reshapes into a male's. He stands on two feet, all tattoos, muscles, and dark brown hair, and kicks the animal toward me. "Here ya go, lazy fucker."

I grab the terrik and crush its bones, spilling the blood into my throat. I'm lapping it up and ripping the meat off the bone while Tash watches me. Moaning, I eat my fill and lick off my teeth before joining him as a male on two feet.

"Dyed your hair again, I see." We both have light hair. Tash likes his dark and keeps dying it.

He looks me up and down and frowns.

"Thanks for the terrik."

"Mmhm." Tash circles me, inspecting my body, sniffing around my shoulder. He sneezes. "You smell…wrong, brother."

That's the poison. "Let's go inside."

Tash throws an arm over my shoulder and nearly collapses my lung when he hits me in the back. "Lost the first span, I hear."

"Depends on what you count as a win."

"What do you mean?" We walk past the pond and take the short path through the forest to emerge in the clearing that leads to his house, a single-story building spanning a large chunk of the property, completely unused by Tash, but I'm fairly certain his two kids will soon run wild through every surface of the unused space.

"How did Vor beat you?" Tash asks.

"Mother poisoned me."

"What?" Tash shouts, making the males on patrol halt in their steps.

I wave at them. "Keep prancing, boys." Chuckling, I continue on toward his house. When my brother doesn't follow, I roll my eyes and walk in reverse. "Don't just stand there, brother. Follow me into Bera's dwelling." His mate is the most worshiped goddess in the lands, Bera, goddess of fertility and war, but I'm not here for his advice, favors, or anything, nor am I here for the goddess. I need to borrow human wisdom, and the human who carries Bera is wise.

Tash's steps echo loudly behind me as we walk toward Tash's bedroom, which is basically the only part of the giant house he uses.

The hall that leads to his bedroom smells of paint. Bera is a famous painter. She levitates near the ceiling, rope tied around her waist. I frown as Tash joins me and opens his mouth.

I lift my finger. "Hold the thought. Why is there a rope tied around Bera's waist?"

"For safety."

"Who are you keeping safe?"

"Just a precaution in case she falls."

"She is a goddess and can levitate." A safety rope sounds stupid to me. Will I get this cautious and stupidly in love with Mae? Nah, I'm gonna die before I get this far with her, and besides, Mae doesn't paint.

"Humans are fragile," Tash says. "If she falls from that height, she can break her neck and die."

"Even prey lands on their feet when they fall."

"Not this prey."

Oh, that's right. Hart mentioned they're uncoordinated. They can fall on their faces and even their sides. Mind-boggling. "Is Bera still talking on the human's back?"

Tash nods. "Imani, Ark is here."

She turns and glides down, then floats across the room on thin air, white eyes crinkling at the corners.

Tash scratches his balls.

I follow along and scratch mine, then my belly, the back of my neck.

Bera stops before me, rises on her toes, and turns up her pretty face. I think she wants to kiss me, and I give her my cheek, keenly aware of my brother's ire.

"How is Lena?" she asks, and folds her hands in front of her. Looking at her now, one would think this female is demure and cute and sings all span like an iseya does in the tree at dawn. One would be fooled.

"Mae is sore between her legs."

Bera laughs. "That a boy."

Tash moves to sit on his throne while Bera leans her elbow on his shoulder. The flimsy cloth she wears slips over her shoulder and falls halfway down her breast, not exposing it, but making a male notice.

Bera could seduce a tree, and I'm only a male with eyes, and my gaze fixes on Bera's big tit. Bera's tits are the stuff of legends. I've prayed to those tits since I was a wee boy. As the legends go, Bera also produces nectar. Right now, the nectar leaks from her nipple and stains the material so there are two wet spots on the shirt, and I stare at them, swallow, thinking about sucking on Mae's tits.

"A pregnant Mae will make nectar," Bera says.

My balls inflate and my cock starts rising.

"Brother, please focus."

I scrub my face. "How do you do it?"

"How do I do what?"

"Not fuck her all the time."

Bera giggles. Her laughter makes my dick even harder. I grab my package and squeeze hard until my eyeballs want to pop out of my head from the pain. My whole body is buzzing. I regret coming here, but I need human wisdom.

"It's a hardship," Tash deadpans, "but someone has to do it."

"Not me, thankfully," I say.

"No, you have it easy. You only have to win the fire

goddess's games, secure the Ra throne, and not die in the process." Tash scrubs his beard. "It smells to me like you're on your way to losing the games and dying in the process."

"It does seem that way."

"I will ask again in case I didn't hear you correctly the first time," he says through his teeth as he leans forward. "What's wrong with you?"

"Mother poisoned me."

Their eyes go wide. I laugh and mock them, widening my eyes before I sit on a log, because Tash is about to lecture me and that shit takes eons.

"How?" Bera asks, looking worried. I appreciate that.

"How is not important. Why is obvious. Where is the antidote is the question."

"What's the poison?" Tash asks.

"Orda."

Tash curses. "Besides Mother, the only other person who knows how to make an antidote is dead."

"Oh no." Bera places a hand over her heart, which just draws my gaze back to her fine tits. The image of pregnant Mae comes to mind again, and with it, leaking nectar from her breasts. On cue, my cock starts leaking seed.

Tash snaps his fingers and points at his eyes. "Look at me, brother. Where do you think she's keeping the antidote?"

"Vor might've had it."

Bera frowns. "Might have had?"

I nod. "He taunted me with a vial, but if I know Mother, and I know her well, she'd have given Vor a tiny bottle of water and not the real thing."

"Because she would fear you'd overpower your little brother and snatch the antidote," Bera says.

Tash and I nod.

"She'll have it somewhere," Tash says. "Her quarters?"

I purse my lips. "Maybe."

"Where would you put it, Ark?" Bera asks. "If it were you, where would you put it?"

"On my person. I wouldn't part from it."

She smiles.

I smile too. "Now all I have to do is snatch it from her."

Tash snickers. "As if that's all you have to do. Mother won't let you near her. And you also have to win Lena's games or die trying."

"Looks like I'm gonna die trying."

Tash and I are pretty realistic, and we both know the odds of winning span two are slim and also that if I don't get the antidote, I'll die. But if I can survive three spans of games and win, I will have more earls in my favor, and during the Ra tribal vote, I'll have a chance of actually becoming the Rai with no blood shed. "I changed my mind. I'll die later," I tell Tash.

"You will die when your time comes, predator," the human says in a voice that sends shivers down my spine. "That time is not now. Now, you will prepare for battle."

Tash scrubs the back of his neck. I think he's got an itch, but is playing it off as if being in the presence of a goddess doesn't affect him.

"The soldiers," I say. "You're preparing to march them somewhere."

Tash nods. "If you lose, Vor will march on my earldom. If you win, we will march on Ralna when they try to kill you."

"The bloodshed is unavoidable," I conclude.

"We will march tonight," Bera says.

"You think I will lose."

"You are unfit," she says. A blush spreads over her pretty face, and she looks down at the floor. "I'm sorry. Sometimes I say things I mean to keep to myself."

Tash's white eyes turn silver. "Unfit."

I growl. "Careful, brother. I can kill you with both hands tied behind my back."

Tash smirks. "Are you sure? Because you didn't kill Vor when you could on the first span of the games."

Because I couldn't and also because Vor is a pussy. "Vor is not a problem," I say.

"Who is the problem, then?" Tash asks.

We stare at each other. I know what I have to do. I've always known, and so has he. I have to take the antidote from my mother's dead body because that's the only way she'll give it to me.

Sighing, I jerk my head toward my house on his property. "Did you get Neri to repair my roof?"

Tash stretches as he stands and shakes his head. "I'll get on it after your games."

"Don't want to waste fixing roofs for a dead male, hm?"

Tash jumps at me and grabs the back of my neck. I let him, even though I hate males in my face. Rubs me all wrong. My brother's eyes are the silver of his hunter, pounding me with his dominance. I smell the thick scent of an Alpha hunter, and it makes me want to rip him to shreds. We both growl, and he says, "Don't talk like that, Ark. You will be Rai."

"Why did you give up the throne for me?" I never asked him that, but he's the eldest. It should be his.

"Because you are the fittest of the Ra, and if I sat as Rai, you would have killed me. It's in the hunter nature. The fittest leads."

I grit my teeth and lie. "I wouldn't have killed you."

Tash brings us chest to chest and holds me there. I'm doing all I can to resist the impulse to bite him. "I gave up the Rai title for a ruthless predator who will do anything to impose his dominance and his rightful place. You're right. You don't have time for dying right now. You hear me?"

He pushes me away right before I snap.

Snarling, I spin and leave his house, then march across the meadow to reach the place I stay when I'm in his earldom. I guess one can call it my house, but it's not my home. My home is in Ralna between Mae's warm thighs.

With Mae's thighs in mind, I kick open the door and head for the basement, where I hoard all the things I've raided and stolen either from Ka, Om, other tribes, or other alien ships during our travels in the universe.

Dresses. Females of Earth, or, as they call themselves, women, like dresses made of flimsy smooth material. I would rather die than put such fabric on my body.

At the portal against the wall, a golden line shimmers, and I touch it at the bottom, then swipe up. The portal opens and shows me the racks and racks of weird alien clothing I'm hoarding. Got it from the pods after the big ship carrying humans exploded.

I have at least thirty dresses, maybe more. Fuck. Picking out a dress or two for Amti was different. I didn't give a fuck if she liked them. While I wanted to bring the female a nice gift, I didn't care if I won because she liked the gift. I was there more to irritate Hart than anything. I sigh, reminiscing about the first games in the Ka territory in decades and the look on Hart's face when he saw me. I snicker and choke, bend over, and start coughing as if my lungs are trying to come out.

Blood hits the floor.

I wipe my mouth and swallow, then stomp over the blood. Better hurry up and win while I'm still alive. "Bera!" I shout. "Come help me pick out a dress!"

Moments pass until I hear Bera's soft steps entering my house. Dust falls on my shoulder as she walks upstairs, then descends via the rope under the house.

"Why are you using the rope when you can glide on air?"

"Habit, I guess. What's up?"

I grab four dresses, different sizes and shapes and colors, but all pretty and clean. "Pick one."

"For whom?" Bera asks.

"Stupid question. Mae, of course."

Bera bats her eyelashes and smiles like a cute little bug. She almost purrs when she says, "The deep green gown. Silk, formfitting, matches her eyes."

I have a feeling Bera is fucking with me. "Are you still mad because I threatened you that one time on the bench?"

"Maybe a little."

"You wouldn't compromise my chances of winning...or would you?"

"I would if you were unfit."

"I am unfit."

"I will determine that, predator."

I shiver, hating when goddesses call me predator. It's demeaning in the tone they say it and also raises my hunter, who aims to serve Bera. If she wanted to, she could pull my strings and make me do her bidding. I can't stand knowing someone other than myself has control of me and mine.

"But," Bera continues, "you are fire blessed already."

"So?"

"So you're also stupid," she deadpans.

"Get out," I say.

She sighs and side-eyes me, her eyes softening and becoming...warm. "You bring out the worst in me, Ark."

"It's a gift. Tell me the problem with the silk green dress that matches Mae's eyes."

"It's not Mae you need to win."

I frown. "What do you mean? Mae chose me, so I have to win her."

"Lena will chose the winner, not Mae."

"Surely they're one and the same."

"Are they?"

"What the fuck, Bera?"

"Or Imani," she says. "One body, one soul, two females intertwined together forever. Please them both and win. Disappoint and...I'll kill you, slowly and painfully."

"Tash!" I shout, my lungs wheezing. "Taaaash. Bera is threatening my life."

"I heard," he says from upstairs, because if Bera is in the basement with me, Tash is not too far from her. I think he's overprotective and ridiculous about her safety, but what do I know about human goddesses? Apparently, and according to Bera, not much of anything.

"You said nobody can threaten anybody under your roof," I remind him.

"No, I said *you* can't threaten her."

"Fuck you too, brother."

"Anytime, brother. Did you pick out your dress?" Laughter booms from his position above. Great, there're more than three males out there listening in while I pick out a dress.

"It's not *my* dress," I grumble.

They laugh.

Bera pats me on the shoulder on her way out. "You'll figure it out."

"Hey, where are you going? We're not done here."

"You still have ways to go." She grabs the rope and rises on her toes.

"Bera, come on."

She lifts off the floor.

"Bera, please."

Pausing, she smiles. "Beg again."

"Please." I am desperate for a dress over here.

"You beg so well," she purrs. "Good luck, predator."

Fuck. I stare at the empty space she vacated and then at the racks of female clothing and all the accessories and trinkets I've stolen over the turns. The green dress is nice, but Bera said no. She said I have to win the human. Lena liked the gloves. What else would she like?

For a long time, I stand there staring at clothes.

This is hard. I need to sit down. Sitting, I prop my elbow on my knee and stroke my braid on my beard, the trunk of trinkets catching my eye.

The night Tash claimed Bera and she consumed us both, we fought, and I tried to kill him, would have killed him if our sister hadn't intervened. The same night, Lena put back the eye Tash had mauled and spent the night with me. I caught her rummaging through the jewels in my trinket trunk.

I kick open the trunk and stare at a million and one pieces of jewelry before me. Which one was it?

Ah, fuck.

CHAPTER SIXTEEN

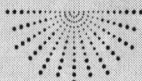

LENA

I spent the duration of the span on the game chair at the top of the palace, where the winds whipped my body and the snowflakes melted over my skin. If it weren't for goddess Mae, I would have frozen solid in these conditions. But her fire burned inside me and continues to burn as the sun goes down and the weather gets even colder.

Tired, thirsty, and hungry, I'm a bit cranky when Dani takes her leave and Feli is free to finally acknowledge me.

Eyes on the controls, he whispers, "The winner will feed you soon."

I whip out my middle finger. *Fuck you, bro.*

When I imagined what my games would be like, I never thought I'd sit all day without food, water, or a friend.

Dani is proving to be a royal heartless bitch. I guess it's to be expected from a woman who offered her own son as a sacrifice for a goddess. Tash escaped the burning pit, but Dani still has another son she could roast.

Thinking of the devil makes her appear back on the terrace. She drinks water from a leather flask. I stare at the flask like it's gonna save my life. My mouth is so parched, my lips are cracked and dry, my cheeks red and stinging from the winds.

"The contestants will be returning shortly," Dani starts, then stands in front of me, her eyes silver, her huntress threatening me. She offers me the flask.

Gripping the armrests so I don't take the water, I shake my head.

"My son Ark can be very charming."

I nod, then lick my cracked lips and glance at the offering of water in her hand.

"But he is unfit for a goddess."

"He seems pretty fit to me." Ark is too proud to display his wounds, and even when he fought Tash and lost an eye, he retreated into his hut. She would know he's unfit because she poisoned him.

A sudden wave of heat warms me. Not just the heat inside my body that's been keeping me warm, but inside my chest. It feels like lava's traveling from my chest down my arms, and my fingertips are starting to burn. Sweat accumulates on my forehead even though it's negative infinity out here and at this high an altitude at the top of the palace.

Dani continues. "Your young heart may indulge itself with Ark, but Mae favors only the fittest. Do you understand what I'm telling you, human?"

"Yes, Dani," I say.

"It is not a question, then, who you will choose to win."

I turn up my palms and rest them on the chair, hoping the vicious wind will cool the burns. Jesus.

"I require an answer," Dani snaps.

"You know, I've looked forward to the games ever since I found out that's what your people did. When Tash held them in his earldom, we girls would sit together and support the prize, make her days go by faster. When I heard my games were to be held in the capital of the biggest tribe in the lands,

I thought it would be a magnificent fun event for me, but all it is…is disappointing." A tiny flame dances over my palm. It disappears as quickly as it came. Did it really happen?

"Mae," Dani whispers and takes a step back.

It did happen! She saw it. "Disappointing," I repeat in a language I can't possibly speak because I've never learned it, but I hear it come out of my mouth, and I know what I'm saying. My voice, it's direct, authoritative, confident, and makes me sit up in my chair and square my shoulders. "You are not taking care of my human."

Dani blinks. "I offered her water. She refused."

Holy crap, I'm having a conversation about me in third person.

"She remains unprotected, hungry, thirsty, and sad." Oh wow, I'm sad? I'm not sad. I'm upset I'm having to sit here all day long by myself. I like to keep the company of good people. I wish my sister was here.

"Forgive me, Mae. I will make amends," Dani says. "What would you have me do?"

Oh, I'm liking this. "Give up the antidote." WHAT?

Dani smiles a wicked smile. "I thought you'd never ask."

There is an antidote. To what? A poison? "Oh my God, of course! You poisoned Ark." I was right to accuse her, but it hadn't occurred to me to ask for the antidote. It's just goes to show how ill-equipped I am to deal with the kind of person Dani is.

Dani crosses her arms over her chest. "I did not."

Lies, Mae whispers in my head, her voice a lover's purr. My nipples perk, and I think Dani's lies excite Mae. I lean forward, flames flaring out of my palms. "Who poisoned him?"

"My other son, Vor."

"And I should pick him this span, I presume?"

"Do you have another fitter choice before you?"

I shrug. "The human enjoys Ark."

No, I don't, I hiss inwardly.

Mae giggles in my head. *Lies. Feed me more lies.*

"And the human can have him as long as you announce my son as winner."

The flames on my palms extinguish, and Dani approaches the chair and says, "Pick Vor and save Ark's life."

∿

The pile of gifts is smaller than it was only yesterday when four hundred predators competed for the right to breed me. Or rather their goddess Mae. This tells me that more than half of the contestants didn't make it back on span two. Are they all poisoned and lying around the land dying? Maybe. I wouldn't put it past Dani to secure Vor's victory by any and all means necessary.

They're competing for you, Mae supplies in my head.

That's not quite true. None of them would be as interested in me if you didn't invade my soul.

Two of them would be interested.

How so, Mae?

Think about it. I haven't spoken to either of them. It's been you, the way you are all along.

You're trying to make me feel better, but the truth is nobody's ever really wanted me, and that's okay because I got used to it and it's been fine all my life, and totally fine if that's the case now too. In fact, wouldn't it be shocking if someone did want me?

Mae falls silent, and I snort. I'm right. She's trying to placate me. Whatever.

"It is time," Dani says and extends a hand.

I clasp it and hold on to her as if she'd offer me support. She wouldn't, but having her by my side as we approach the pile of gifts on the terrace is oddly comforting. At the front of the pile, I recognize a thick golden band decorated with colorful precious stones. The stones aren't perfectly polished, but still raw and wild and glued on the band to make something unique and beautiful. That's the piece of jewelry I liked from Ark's chest.

Careful not to damage it, I step over it and pick up Vor's tiara.

"Good choice," Dani says and secures the tiara on my head.

I turn up my palm, and she raises an eyebrow.

I roll my eyes. "The antidote."

"You haven't announced a winner yet."

"Obviously, I have." I point to the tiara on my head. A symbol of rule. Vor's rule. He's telling his people he'll become their new Rai.

Dani scoffs. "After you announce the winner."

Heat rushes up my body, and I feel like I'll combust.

Dani must've sensed the change in my body temperature because she yanks the vial she's been wearing as a pendant on the necklace tucked between her breasts and hands it to me.

I walk up to the terrace and stand there watching the sun set while the predators chant Vor's name.

"I chose Vor," I say with as much conviction as I can muster and turn away so I don't accidentally find Ark in the masses. In my rooms, I take a sip of yesterday's water before collapsing on the bed.

Vor. It's gonna be Vor who claims me tonight.

~

A hand over my mouth wakes me from a light sleep.

Ark's painted his face half red, half black, his eyes are silver, and he's poised above me, part of his features in hunter, part remaining in male. It's some sort of half-transition state I've never seen before on a predator. He's half male, half hunter, and my heart's gonna beat out of my chest.

Ark leans in, his face sprouting fur as he does. "I didn't want to start a war, but I will now."

I shake my head.

His hand sneaks between my legs, and he parts them, strokes me there, wants to make me wet.

Where is Vor? It's nighttime, and Vor should be here, so he must be around the corner of my chambers or at least on his way. He'll engage Ark when he finds him here fingering me. He'll strangle me. For sure, I'm gonna die.

Ark sticks a finger into my pussy. I groan and push my hips up. He removes his hand from my mouth to hold my wrists above my head as his thickness enters me, making me gasp. He fucks me like he hates me, long angry strokes that make me want to scratch out his eyeballs and scream for more at the same time.

I raise my hips and meet him halfway, lifting my face to try to kiss him. His silver eyes and almost completely furry face tell me he's hanging on to his male form by a thread.

"I couldn't let you die," I say as an excuse for not picking him.

"Shut up," he hisses, then kisses my lips, lingering, and grazes my cheeks, nose, one eyelid.

"You shut up. I have the antidote."

Ark's not listening. He's pistoling into me as if he's trying to live inside me. When he lets go of my arms, I hug him tightly, press my cheek to his, and whisper, "You are mine, predator."

He presses a hand over my mouth. "Lies," he says and fucks me. "You picked another male."

"I know, but I had to. I made a deal with Dani."

"All the lies." He smiles, and it reminds me of his mother and the cunning smiles she sends my way.

"What will you do?" I ask.

He grabs my hip and pushes it down so I can't move, then starts pumping into me fast. I grab his biceps and hold on, hitching breaths until Ark throws back his head and his movement halts. "The hook is yours," he grits out. "Take it!" Jets of seed rush inside me, and I feel the force as his cock pumps it inside me.

I'm so close.

I reach down and rub my clit so I can ride out this moment with him, and blissfully sigh once I come.

Ark leaps off the bed, leaving me empty. Uncertain about his intentions, I grab the fur and pull it over my breasts, then sit up in bed, my hair falling over my shoulder.

Ark stands by the bed, fists on his hips. "Fucking you is far better than consuming you. If I consumed you, then you'd be gone, and that would make me sad."

I pull the sheet over my mouth, embarrassed heat crawling up my cheeks. I'm not sure why I'm embarrassed. "Good thing you figured that out. Also…" I pause to roll over and reach under the mattress and grab the antidote. It's gone. "Oh no," I whisper and jolt out of bed. Crouching beside the mattress, I stick my hand under it and across the floor and sweep the length of it.

Ark comes around and holds up the empty vial.

Standing, I throw up my hands. "Could've told me you got it."

"It was water."

I gape.

"Not to worry," he says. "Vor came and delivered the real thing."

There's a moment where my brain is trying to process

what Ark said, and once that's done, my body reacts with fear. I rush out of my sleeping quarters and into the living space, where I find the body of a gray-and-black hunter with his tongue hanging out.

I clamp my mouth shut with both hands before glancing back at Ark.

The cold white eyes of a male predator are watching me, reading my reactions.

"Who is that?" I whisper, and also then realize Ark fucked me violently but quietly. He's hiding. We're not supposed to get discovered here. I am another male's prize for the night. Oh. This is wrong, and I feel Mae inside me burning with thoughts and heating up my body, but I can't clear my own thoughts long enough to hear what she wants or says.

"You know who that is."

"I need you to say it." I've never seen Vor's hunter. Maybe it's not him. Maybe there's a chance...

"It's Vor."

I gasp. "What have you done?"

"I killed him," Ark says as if stating he's going out for a hunt. "Kept it clean so as not to make a mess." He moves his arms in a way that mimics the snapping of an animal's neck.

"Have you lost your mind?!" I screech, and he's on me in a second, a palm over my mouth again.

"Did you really expect me to accept defeat?"

I shake my head.

"What did you think was going to happen after you chose him?" Ark removes his hand so I can answer.

"I thought Vor would come and claim me. I thought you would...understand. I wasn't really thinking about much of anything besides trying to save your life."

Ark closes his eyes for a second, and when he opens them again, they're silver. In a rough sandpaper voice, he says, "For as long as I breathe, I would never give you up. Never."

"Oh boy," I mutter. "Gonna let your words sink in for a minute here."

Ark frowns. "How long will that take?"

"A minute."

Ark keeps staring at me, leaning in.

"What?" I ask.

"Has it sunk in yet?"

"No, not yet."

He nods. "You have all night to think about my words."

"We need to disappear," I say, done thinking about anything else.

Ark cracks his neck and stretches, appearing mighty relaxed when he should be freaked the fuck out.

"We bail and never return," I prompt him again. "Obviously."

His smile reaches his eyes. "Obviously."

I nod. "Let's go."

He snatches me and kisses me and makes me open my mouth so he can shove his fat tongue inside and purr and make me want him again. I can't keep my wits about me when he's around, and I kiss him back, my palms sliding down his sides. I pause at the now-closed wound and tap it.

Ark breaks the kiss with a growl. "Human," he hisses. "Let's stay and fuck again."

CHAPTER SEVENTEEN

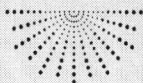

ARK

Mother was never going to give up Mae. It didn't matter if I won the games fair and square, mother identified the goddess as the guaranteed must-have item for whoever ascended as Rai. She might even have used Vor's affection for the female and pushed him into death at my hands. I wouldn't know for sure because, while ruthless, she can also be a loving mother.

She used to be.

She would pour all her might into raising us. Perhaps what she used to give Kore, Tash, and me, she now gives Vor, and in that case, she will grieve not only for the throne, but for her son as well.

Mother also knows I would never give up seeking the throne. What she didn't know was that if she pushed me into a corner as she has with the poison, I'd mark the goddess so Vor can't breed her.

Nobody besides me can breed Mae now.

Relieved, I kick the log out of the circular formation in the living space. It rolls across the room and hits Vor's body. I turn up the log with my foot and sit on it.

Mae kicks a log and says, "*Ouch*" before hopping on one foot and sitting across from me on the floor. She leans in, green eyes wide and curious. "What kind of a ritual are you going to perform?"

"Hm?"

"The ritual. You look all detached and determined… It's a ritual, isn't it?"

"I'm going to flay him now."

Mae's mouth opens before she says, "Besides that being one of the most fucked-up things I've heard in a while, flaying would take a long time, and I have a feeling we need to get out of here."

"You will wear him for the last span of the games."

"I will not."

I get the dagger out and grab Vor's ears.

Mae jumps off the log. "Wait."

I look up. "Yes?"

"I won't wear his fur. Are you crazy?"

"Slightly." I slice the thick hunter coat and slide the blade under it.

"Ark, please listen to me."

"I'm listening."

"But you're still carving him up!" The fire from the pits flares, and the flames crawl up the walls.

I look around. "That a girl. When I'm done, I'm gonna fuck you up against the flaming wall."

"Get serious."

"I am serious."

"Ark, please." Mae kneels next to me, a small hand on my forearm.

I stare at it, lift it up, and kiss the top of it. "You are scared?"

"Terrified."

"Of?"

"Your mother and what she's gonna do when she finds out Vor's dead."

"I will tell you what she will do. She'll be sad and then mad. But not as enraged as she will be when she figures out my plan."

"What's your plan?"

"I marked you."

The hook is yours. When he said it during sex, I heard him, but my foggy middle-of-the-night brain couldn't process the significance of the mating until now. "Marked me with your hook?"

I nod.

"You haven't won the games yet. And you're not supposed to mark females."

"You're not a female. You're the patron goddess of my tribe."

"That probably makes marking me worse."

"It does."

"You didn't ask permission."

"For what?"

"To mark me."

"I will ask for forgiveness."

Mae snorts. "God, Ark, you win the asshole medal."

"Thank you, sweets, because I lost the games. Vor won two of the three nights."

"The third day of the games counts. Tash told me the rules. A loser can win on day three. The odds weren't in your favor, but there was a chance."

"My mother gave you water, not the real antidote. I had to take it from him."

"If you told me it was water, I would have stolen the vial while Vor slept."

I pause, gritting my teeth. "While he slept in your bed?"

Mae swallows, but doesn't answer.

I jab the dagger into his dead body.

"Ark, please, we have to get out of here."

I continue skinning my little brother. "Why would we need to do that?"

"Because you just killed Dani's son. You know, a....a prince, a future king of the Ra."

"Good, Mae, good. And if I killed the prince, who then gets the throne?"

"You? Is it you? Is this what everything is about? The stupid throne?" Mae gets up and stomps away. She returns with her tiara and throws it at my head.

I duck.

The torches fall to the ground, and fire spreads over the floor and encircles us. Mae's red hair lifts, and flames lick her skin.

Fuck, Mae is sexy when she's mad. I regret nothing. Even if it costs me my life, I regret nothing. I marked her, and she will have my pups, and one of them, one span when I am long gone, will rule the Ra. Tash and Bera will take care of Mae, so I've got nothing to lose, and I'm definitely not running or hiding.

"I didn't kill him for the throne," I tell her. "I killed him because he came here to breed you, and the thought of that made me murderous. I don't know any other way to express how I feel about you."

"Oh my," she whispers.

"What?" I yank the fur I sliced on this side so it tears off the skin completely.

"You have feelings you want to express."

"Yeah, I got those." I flip his body so I can get to his other flank. The dead body thumps on the floor. I grab the leg and pull it to me, positioning it so I can dig in again from this side. "I'm feeling pretty fucking great right now. And I need you to be brave and, more importantly, stand with me. You think you can do that, Mae?"

"Do I have a choice?"

"You do."

"What is it?"

"Burn Ralna to ashes and assume your throne. You're marked and seeded and will have pups."

"And what about you?"

"A goddess doesn't need a male."

"But I will rule alone, then," she says.

"You will have Bera."

"No."

I chuckle. "Don't worry, I'm hard to kill." Looking up, I wink, but Mae's eyes, filled with tears, make me drop Vor's fur. I wipe my hands on my ierto and tap my knee. "Come here, Lena."

She folds into my lap, and I tuck her close. If I could, I would tuck her into me and keep her humanity inside me until the storm that the new span will bring has passed.

Mae buries her nose into the crook of my neck and inhales loudly.

My cock's hard as a rock. I reach between us and adjust myself, then clear my throat.

She chuckles. "How can you be horny right now?" She's quiet, content to sit here with me, and I am…also content to sit with her. It reminds me of the night we spent together, content in each other's company. She asks for nothing, I realize, while I want to give her everything.

"Tell me a story," she says.

"A funny story? Sexy story? No, never mind. I'm not telling any sexy stories."

"A story about Dani."

I scrub my beard, and she takes it and strokes the braid

there, then starts rearranging the beads while I tell her a story of my mother and all her lies.

"After my father passed away, Mother grieved. She grieved for several cycles, maybe even an entire turn, during which earls came and went from the palace seeking favors and sex from her. During most of that period, Tash and I used to run around the forests and fields in hunter, but as the males kept coming for Mother, we stopped dicking around the fields and sat with her more, worried someone would try to hurt her and snatch the power from the family."

Mae looks up from playing with the beads in my hair. "And?"

"It wasn't until turns later that we came to realize Mother had invited the earls into the palace as suitors, and from those suitors she picked the one she'd favor in the games, and only then did she announce her own games." I chuckle. "Mother even ran the controls."

"What happened after the games?"

I glance at Vor's pretty face. Even his hunter is handsome. "To secure the earl's position and her own, she then had to get rid of her previous mate's children, and she tried to do so as if we weren't hers." Mother did spare Kore from assassins, but Kore wouldn't extend the same courtesy to Mother. If given the opportunity, she'd stab Mother in the eye and not blink.

"The most prominent power shift in Ralna started after Vor was born, and Tash and I became stepsons to a male who would sometimes beat us and put us in the holes. Still young and weak, neither of us could defend ourselves. Often I wonder why our stepfather didn't kill us while he still could."

"Perhaps Dani wouldn't let him."

"Yeah, but not for noble reasons. I think we were her backup plan in case the male she chose in the games didn't work out the way she planned. After all, Tash and I were born and bred of the fittest bloodlines, and those are necessary to rule the Ra tribe."

"She hates you, Ark."

"Mmhm. She sees herself in me."

"I see it too."

"Thank you," I deadpan.

Mae brushes her lips over my neck. I've never had another person this close to my jugular, and by choice. I don't even know if I'd show my jugular to my brother Tash or my sister, and I trust those two with my life.

"So when did you try to take her down?"

I laugh and tickle her for asking the right questions and knowing that's what I did. "After I battled a Ka warlord and won, I skinned his hunter and brought the fur to my stepfather. Mother viewed it as a threat. The idiot viewed it as a gift, which is precisely why he's dead and she's not."

This was also around the same time I proposed a peace treaty with the Ka.

Laughter followed me out of the council room as I left, mad as fuck at everyone for wanting to sacrifice more Ra lives for Ka land. Fuck the Ka land. We got plenty of land. So what if it's a little cold in most parts of the Ra world? Since when did my people need to bathe in the sun and rest by the sand?

Tash, though, he followed me out of the council meeting, and we never looked back, effectively splitting the loyalties of the tribe. While I worked outside Ralna, Mother worked inside it, and she outsmarted me, outnumbered me, and I hadn't even realized she'd dragged other tribes into our family throne dispute.

They're here. The other tribes. Just waiting for the signal to move into Ralna.

I gave them an excuse.

They're gonna flood the streets of the city with the blood of my people.

Because I killed her son, the male who would deliver on whatever riches Mother promised them. I bet it was Ka land. Maybe even Om land. We are conquerors, warriors. It's in our blood to barter with land that's not ours to give.

Mae asks no more questions, and I hold her until the sun rises over the city and the noise of the gathering crowds brings us back to reality.

CHAPTER EIGHTEEN

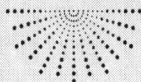

ARK

*M*ae is wearing nothing. Her body is exquisite, her hair the color of fire. She is perfect in every way and I don't deserve her, but I marked her anyway because I am a selfish motherfucker and I do not share anything with anyone. Not the throne. Not the land. Not the friendship with the Alpha and leader of the Ka tribe, and certainly not my pretty prey who is the goddess of lies.

I believe every word that falls from her lips.

I wish she would lie more.

I wish she would lean into Mae's lies, for then she would survive and thrive in case I'm not around to protect her.

She walks to the door that leads onto the terrace.

Any moment now, she'll stride outside smelling of me and of Vor's blood.

At first, nobody will be the wiser. She'll wave at the contestants as I asked her to and pretend everything is fine, until Mother starts wondering where Vor is and why he hasn't joined her on the terrace yet.

In the chambers, the fire rages, and I wonder why the guards haven't knocked on the door. I wonder what Vor instructed them to do last night. Did he remove them from their posts for the night? Or at least move them far enough away that they can't hear inside Mae's chambers?

Or was it Mae's raging fire that muted the sounds of Vor's neck snapping. It was a clean kill. I didn't want him to suffer. It pains me that I had to kill him, but I knew I'd rather have him die than let him touch my female.

I grab the small leather pouch from my sack, then pour the contents into the fire. Mae spins around. "A prayer to Bera?" she asks and approaches me. I know I'm talking to Mae, the goddess, directly. It creeps me out.

"I'm going to war," I say.

Mae smiles, flames dancing in her green eyes. There's also madness and anger, and I want my human back. I do pray to Mae. I love Mae and all the goddesses, but I don't want to speak with them or look at them directly, and I definitely don't want to succumb to their influence and become Mae's tool that she uses whenever she needs to and discards when she doesn't.

Gently, I press a palm over her cheek and kiss her nose.

The fire in her eyes dims and disappears, returning to the forest-green color I'm going to miss now that I've marked her. All the marked humans have white eyes like us. The white membrane over the eyes allows them to see the portals, and I presume in the spans to come, Mae will visit many parts of Ra lands. My people will welcome her with open arms.

"It is time," I say.

Mae nods.

The moment she opens the terrace doors, I snap into kill mode.

The wind gushes inside, picking up the already strong fire inside the rooms and the sky where the roof used to be. It's positively roaring with life. Below, people cheer and hoot, looking forward to span three of the games where the winner takes the prize. They expect a feast, maybe even an audience with their goddess.

They'll get a war.

Bera promised there would be a battle, and she will damn well get one.

I never imagined I'd start a war inside my own tribe or that I'd yearn for a female so much, I felt compelled to mark her. I blame the marking urge on Hart. Yup, it's all Hart's fault. Had he not marked Amti, no one after him would mark their females, and the madness wouldn't have started spilling all over the tribal lands.

Stopping at the threshold before venturing outside, Mae turns, the wind lifting her hair, framing her pretty face. She's scared but smiles, puts on a happy face so my mother doesn't notice anything is amiss just yet.

I nod. "Tell her lies."

Mae walks onto the terrace, and her people roar.

CHAPTER NINETEEN

···············

LENA

*T*he noise out here is deafening. Fire rages over the blue skies, the chamber walls, the floors, and even at my heels. Mae's power feels like a drumming pulse in my body, making my fingertips tingle. I expect to shoot fire out of my nails any second now, so I fist my hands and keep them at my sides.

Her back to me, Dani stands at the railing, waving at the people, clueless to the fact her son lies dead inside my chambers. Clueless now, but not for long. Any minute now, Ark's gonna show up here with me, and Dani's gonna go crazy. Then all hell will break loose. She's gonna kill us both. *Mae?* I call to the goddess.

She stays silent. No help there.

Slowly, I attempt to walk toward Dani, but my knees shake violently, and I almost trip over my own feet. Better stay in place and wait for her to wonder why I haven't reached her yet and greeted the contestants and the people.

At first, she turns her profile, a clear invitation to join her, and when I don't, she turns her head slightly more, locking those white eyes with mine. A frown forms on her face, and she walks slowly toward me, then stops dead in her tracks.

Growling ensues behind me, and I swallow hard, trembling. I can feel Ark's hunter behind me before he comes to stand beside me.

"What is this?" Dani asks.

Ark is in hunter, so he's elected not to speak, and I can't find my voice. Like a fish, my mouth opens and closes. I don't have the courage to tell her what happened last night.

Low at the back of her throat, Dani growls at Ark.

A keening noise escapes me.

The people below have quieted. In the periphery of my vision, I catch Feli placing a hand on his dagger. I don't know if he'll slay me or save me. He can't save me. Nobody can.

In hunter, Ark is a massive seven-foot gray creature. He circles me slowly, growling so loudly that I might just pee from fear. Dani steps forward, and Ark snaps his tail right in front of her.

"What have you done?" she asks through gritted teeth.

Ark lifts his leg and sprays my thigh. Once done, he continues circling while I stare down at the urine sliding down my calf. I can't believe he just pissed on me.

"You pissed on my leg," I state. "Wha…"

Ark grunts and sits beside me, his massive body leaning into mine and nudging me. I glance at the creature eyeing me from the corner of his eye. He drops his head and nudges my waist. I think he wants me to pet him. My hand shakes as I run it through the fur over his neck and back. Coarse, prickly, strong hairs. Definitely not a Yorkie.

Dani rounds us and rushes inside.

I'm glued in place, but Ark isn't. He snaps his tail and strides to the edge of the terrace, then rises on the rail with his front paws. Massive back muscles flex as he leans forward and roars.

129

You could hear a pin drop in the city of thousands.

From the chambers, Dani releases a bloodcurdling cry.

It wakes me from my stupor, and I panic. I start running toward Ark, who takes the moment of Dani's shock to return to his male form. He spreads his arms, and I run into them, seeking reassurance and protection.

He runs his claws through my hair. "You will survive this. Trust me."

"Will you?" I look up.

"Does it matter?"

"It matters."

His silver eyes soften as his gaze roams my face.

"What?" I ask. "What are you thinking?"

He remains quiet, then glances behind him. I go around him and gasp. Predators are fighting on the streets. The market I've visited every day since I arrived in Ralna is covered in blood body parts. Dani's still in the chambers, which worries me.

The contestants start scaling the palace walls, and Ark takes out a dark ball, the same object he used to disappear. "Last piece," he says. "Can only transport one person." He grabs me by the back of my neck and kisses me before throwing the ball. Ark's hands slide to my shoulders and he grips them, trying to push me into the portal. I clutch his belt and hold on tight.

"No!" I scream.

"Mae, let go. You'll hurt yourself." Ark's trying to shake me off, but I'm holding on to him tightly. This was his plan all along. He'd save me and sacrifice himself. Did Mae ask him for a sacrifice? Did Bera? Fuck them both. "I'm not leaving you." I know what it feels like to abandon someone. God knows, people have done it to me all my life, and I'm not gonna do the same to the only man who sets my soul on fire.

The tiny portal hole in space shimmers. Ark snarls and grabs my wrists, tries to detach me.

"I'm not leaving you," I cry out.

He could yank me off him if he wanted to, but I don't think he wants to hurt me. His strength can rip off my arms.

Something flies past me and nicks both our cheeks.

Ark envelops me in his arms, keeping me safe from harm. Turning my head, I see Dani at the chamber's entrance, a bow and arrow aimed at us.

"Why won't you listen to me, Mae?" Ark whispers.

"Because I'm not just Mae."

"Your heart is gonna get you killed." Slowly, he puts me behind him and takes out his daggers. He crouches, assuming his battle stance. The growling noises he makes in his chest are those of his hunter.

I glance behind us at the same time as a male climbs onto the terrace and snatches my elbow. He starts screaming in pain and kneels, hand still attached to my elbow while his arm melts until it falls off, severed from the body.

Flames spread over the railing and surround us. The fire burns high and bright, and the males from below that were climbing stop at the railing, snarling at the flames they can't jump over.

A predator lands near us.

It's not a male. It's Kore, Ark's sister. She flips her hair behind her shoulder and takes out a shield and a thick broadsword.

Dani laughs. "An army of two." She puts away her bow and arrow and claps. "Bravo, Ark. Master strategy to take over the throne."

"It's not over until Bera whistles," Ark says.

"Bera is not here, and she will not come for a weakling like you."

"She will come for Mae."

"This is not Mae," Dani screams. "This is a pathetic human I should've consumed when I had the chance. But no," she spits. "Vor wanted the girl, and look where that got him and you and all of us. Pathetic." Dani turns to the army pouring through my chambers and standing behind her. "During the games, Ark killed the winner and publicly marked our patron goddess. These offenses mean death."

"Kill, kill, kill," the males chant and start beating their axes against their shields.

"Do you have a shield?" I whisper to Ark.

"No, baby, I don't have a shield."

"Why not? Everyone else has one."

"I don't fight with a shield."

"Why not?" I'm panicking again.

"The shield slows me down."

"Oh God, there's two of you and a hundred of them."

"There's more than a hundred," Kore pitches in.

"So nice of you to join me, sister," Ark says, and I detect sarcasm.

"I was out of town. What's the plan, brother?"

"He doesn't have one," Dani says. "He killed my son on the back of madness and lust."

"Amti, Amti, Amti," the males chant.

"And Bera will not favor a fool. Seize them!"

Males rush us, but the fire on the roof folds over them like a relentless wave of lava, melting them underneath. Screaming, engulfed in fire, the few escapees run around the terrace, where Kore and Ark slay them.

More males pour out of the chambers and onto the terrace and over the railing. Some catch on fire, but not all. My entire body is burning, and when other males try to grab me, their arms fry and fall off.

Ark's fighting with all his might, his movements agile. Never too far from me, he dances with his swords, flipping, rolling, jumping, stabbing, and slicing. It's both beautiful and savage, and I think he might kill them all.

I think that until he's midleap and an arrow flies into his neck. Ark lands on his feet, but wobbles back and forth. Taking the arrow, he breaks it with a snarl. I rush to him and hug his body.

Another arrow nicks my cheek and pierces his chest.

I close my eyes and wait for the arrow that's gonna go through both of us.

"Yield," Dani orders behind me, her voice calm and collected, which scares the crap out of me. "The next one will go through her belly."

Ark remains quiet. "Is she lying?" he whispers. "Does she really mean to hurt you?"

I swallow. "You're not listening, Ark. She means to hurt you. Yield."

"Never," he says to me.

"Yield, predator," I say in the ancient tongue. "You can't protect the human if you're dead. Yield."

The silver in his eyes dims and disappears, replaced by the white of a male. "I yield," he says, his voice gurgling.

"Louder, Ark. They can't hear you over the fire."

"I yield!" Ark shouts, blood spouting from his mouth. Will he survive these wounds?

CHAPTER TWENTY

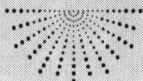

ARK

*T*he hole is a dark and lonely place where hunters pace in a circle until they either starve or go mad from being confined in a small space. I'll die before I go mad, for Mother pierced my lung and my throat, so I'm having a hard time breathing, and while I can heal wounds quickly, I am not immortal.

I presume Tash is marching on Ralna with Bera, goddess of war, and my mother spoke the truth when she said Bera won't favor a fool. Bera, like all our goddesses, favors the fittest, and that means I can't die. I think I'll live by the sheer force of my will and spite. I will live in spite of my mother.

After I yielded, Mae took over the human completely and simply walked away as if I didn't exist. Mae favors the strongest, the fittest, and I have proven unfit time and time again.

One arrow pierced my throat and the other my chest, preventing the change to hunter, so I'm stuck on two feet, unable to heal faster. I lie on the wet ground, counting the stars in the sky instead of watching the fire Mae created above her chambers. The nights spent with her were the best of my life, and to preserve my sanity for as long as possible while Mother leaves me rotting in this hole, I'll think only of Mae and her smile and those pretty green eyes that I'm sure have turned white by now.

I've lain here slowly dying for five spans, going on six tonight, and yet I won't die. Perhaps Bera and the other goddesses have other plans for me that don't include dying in a rotten hole. Perhaps, perhaps.

At least I don't have to drive myself crazy with thoughts of my mother reopening the games for Mae. She is a marked female, unable to breed with another. This also means Mae holds the future of our bloodline, and if I were my mother (often, we do think alike), I'd keep Mae for as long she's pregnant, then get rid of the female as soon as the pups come out of her. Mother will raise them as her own, train them, and have heirs that will do her bidding.

She will exterminate the Ka and find a way to either gain favor with Bera or slay her outright.

It is unfortunate the human females are fragile, much more fragile and killable than our own females, and it makes me wonder why the goddesses chose them over our females in the first place. They're unfit and small, and they listen to their hearts way too much.

I scratch my balls.

Perhaps that's where they draw their strength from. Perhaps that's why the goddesses chose them over our females, who have grown bitter and nasty as the turns passed and they couldn't conceive. Have our females stopped praying to Bera? I know Kore hasn't, but Kore is not the rule. She's the exception, for she is a warrior through and through.

I don't have all the answers, but I can ponder them all span long until I breathe out my last breath. Which is likely to be at dawn.

I hitch a breath as blood continues accumulating in my lungs.

Something above me stirs.

A terrik?

Oh, yummy.

Trying to rise and claw at the hole's walls, I whine. I can't move. My lungs aren't working.

A length of rope drops down the hole.

I blink, unsure if I'm seeing correctly.

"Psst," sounds from above.

I blink again, trying to clear my blurry vision. Hart's hairy ass flashes as he descends the rope.

"I could've died without seeing your ass."

"You will die anyway." Hart, the Alpha of the Ka tribe, lands next to me and crouches, taking stock of my wounds. "How are you even alive?"

"Out of sheer spite for my mother."

He nods. "Word has it you killed Vor but didn't ascend to the Rai."

I nod.

Hart scrubs his beard. "Who do you think will ascend?"

"My pups, when they're ready." I cough out blood and groan, glaring at the Ka asshole. "By all means, Hart, pull up a log and let's chat. Can I offer you a drink? Smoke? Motherfucker."

Hart smiles, the orange eyes of his hunter flashing. "I like seeing you in a helpless state."

"You've come to gloat?" If I die, Mother will come after the Ka with all her might, and because the Ka hold several goddesses and Bera walks with the Ra, the conflict between them will awaken the goddess of doom, and we shall all perish at twilight.

Hart ties the rope around my waist. "This is gonna hurt."

"Nah." Someone yanks me up, and it feels like my spine

splits in half. They're dragging me out of the hole, and I'm trying not to wail in pain as my lungs collapse, my throat closes, and darkness consumes me.

～

Groggy from sleeping too long, I scrub my eyes before stretching on…Hart's bed. He smells like ass, but there's a pleasant scent of prey and a newborn pup here too, and I inhale a lungful. It makes me think of my human and how she smells like both food and fucking and nights spent cuddling by the fire.

A sharp pain pierces my lungs, and I snap open my eyes. I look down to see a healed wound, a tiny scar next to all the other scars on my chest. I rub my chest, but the pain won't go away.

"Aww, are you lovesick?"

I look up. It's Nar, the male who skinned the most Ra in the wars. Goddess, I can't stand him, and I don't dignify his question with an answer. Groaning, I sit up, and the pain slices my chest again. I hit my chest and growl. "What is this?"

"Those are feelings," Nar says.

"What?"

"Feelings, motherfucker. You lost your hook and gained feelings in the chest."

"I didn't lose my hook."

"It's not attached to your dick," he says as he slices off a piece of terrik. My mouth waters.

"You've been staring at my dick?"

"Yeah."

I smirk. "Did it make you feel small?"

Nar snorts. "Hey, everyone, the asshole is alive and well." He throws a terrik leg at my head. I don't duck. I catch it and gnaw at it like the starving predator I am. Pausing, I realize a Ka male hunted for me and fed me. I'll never live this down.

Several portals open at once, and Ka males pile into the room, surrounding the bed, making me edgy and wanting to snap. But then I detect the familiar scent of a Ra female. It's my sister. "Kore?"

"Here, brother." She pushes her way through the males guarding me and sits on the bed to kiss my forehead.

"Awww," Nar says.

"How are you feeling?" she asks.

I open my mouth to answer, but Nar says, "He's lovesick."

Laughter booms in the room.

I sniff. "You smell like Tash. Is he here?" I ask my sister.

She nods. "We're ready whenever you are, so stop being a lazy pussy and get dressed. We have a land to conquer and a Rai to make." She dumps a sack into my lap.

I rummage through it. "I almost died," I tell her. Not lazy.

"Excuses, excuses."

I look up from the sack, and my sister winks.

Slowly, I stand and shake my head to clear it, then dress in the iertos made for a Rai. A formal Rai uniform for when a Rai goes to battle. White on white, with red precious-metal plates decorating the three belts I stacked over my torso. Still, my chest hurts, and I sit down, hitting my rib cage on both sides. "How long have I been here?"

"Seven spans."

Too long. How is Mae? I want to ask, but my throat constricts as if there's a rock inside there. Instead, I ask, "Why haven't I healed yet?"

"You have." Hart's booming voice precedes him as he enters the room. With a jerk of his head, he dismisses everyone and sits beside me. We stare at what looks like a tree growing from a large pot filled with dirt.

"There is a tree in your room," I say.

"Flowers make Amti happy."

I side-eye him. "Has nobody ever told you that you can pick each flower and make a bundle for Amti, instead of having to dig up trees?"

He side-eyes me and deadpans, "No, nobody told me that and I would not know if it wasn't for you, oh Ark of tree wisdom."

"I saw Lena do it once is all." In my chest, my heart flips or something. I don't know what this is! There is something wrong with my heart. "I didn't heal right. In here." I point at my chest. "What did you do to me?" It's Hart's fault. It's always and forever all Hart's fault.

He smiles. "Do you want to know how Mae is doing?"

"No."

"Do you miss her?"

"No."

He chuckles. "Tell her all the lies."

I chuckle too. I miss her and I love her and I want to be beside her and I'm sorry I'm not.

Hart and I sit there for a bit, neither of us speaking. It takes me back to that one time after the battle of Sinue where we lay in mud, wounded and exhausted from fighting all night, trying to kill each other.

"You will be Rai," he says. "Or we shall all perish." Hart will help me ascend, because if he doesn't, the Ka tribe will be no more. "My Amti is dreaming of Aimea of doom and twilight."

"I thought about Aimea too."

He nods. "We all have."

Silence resumes as we mentally prepare for what's to come when I arrive in Ralna with the Ka.

"I smelled my brother."

"He's here." Hart stands and cracks his neck. "So is Bera.

Hurry up, Ark. The males are restless, and Eme is itching to bleed some Ra." He winks.

"Spare as many of my males as you can."

Hart snorts.

I stand and grab him by the shoulders. "Swear on Amti, or I won't march with you."

"I swear it, but if Bera whistles, only a few will survive."

I nod. "You're not bringing Amti?"

"No."

Thank the fine tits for that. Amti creeps me out, and I can't believe I competed for her, almost won her. Inwardly, I shudder.

Hart stands by his portal controls.

"Where is Mas?" That's his portal master, the best one in the lands, and we will need him.

"In Ralna."

"With Eme?" Of blood and grace.

"Mmhm. She wouldn't miss a good butchering of predators." He walks through the open portal. On the other end of the portal stands a Ra army of several hundred males. They cheer when they see me.

"You coming?" Hart asks.

I smile showing all my teeth and step through the portal. Turning, I close it and inhale the scent of aggression, my eyes fluttering at the beauty of it. "It's been a while since we battled," I say.

The males bang their weapons against the metal on their belts.

"It's been never since we fought side by side with the Ka." I walk in front of the line of males, looking for my brother.

The males continue banging their weapons against the metal. "My mother has led us into war after a war, and I'm tired of dying for Ka land."

The males fall silent, and I stop, making eye contact with

as many of them as I possibly can. "That's right. Fuck Ka land."

The Ka army behind Hart boos.

I wave them off. "We are Ra, and we have plenty of land. So it's a little cold, a little frozen in parts, a little bloody over in the Blood Dunes." I pause as they laugh. The Blood Dunes belong to Eme, who mated a Ka portal master and effectively claimed a piece of Tash's land. Nobody goes there because the sands are cursed. "But it's a lot of land! We are the largest tribe on Nomra Prime."

My males hoot.

I lift a finger. "And yet, we have not had a Rai in many turns. This has hurt us, divided us, and made us weak. Our Ka neighbors have portal technology we do not. We can trade."

"We craft nice jewelry so you Ra can finally look pretty, maybe snatch a goddess or two," Nar says.

"The Ra need no more goddesses," a soft female voice says.

Bera walks up, and the males go silent. She's wearing a thick gold necklace matching the circular plates covering her large nipples, leaving her breasts bare. There is a reason why my people swear by Bera's fine tits. At the top of her head, a golden crown sits upon an elaborate golden head wrap.

I scratch my belly, the back of my neck, my balls. The goddess of war is most powerful in the company of an army. She stops beside me and strokes my brother, whom she intends to ride into battle. Her body is beautifully painted with swirls and feminine curves using only three colors. Red, black, and white. I admire the war paint and wonder if she will honor me and paint me, give me a piece of divine blessing as we head out.

Tash in hunter growls as I approach Bera and place a hand on her belly.

141

"You've never looked sexier," I tell her.

Bera blushes, and I know she's still a woman and not entirely consumed by our fierce goddess. Oddly, that makes me happy. I do think these women, with their feelings and hearts, have added kindness to our brutal ways, and I want the same for my Mae. I want the human. I want Lena, and I will damn well have her.

Bera grabs the back of my head and slaps a palm full of red paint on one side of my face, then smears the rest of the paint on my brother's fur. Thunder strikes, the sky above us instantly darkening. "Predator," she says. "Too many goddesses walk the lands, and they've stirred the one that shall not be allowed to walk. But the twilight of doom is upon us. I have faith that you will deliver us from Aimea's evil."

I peck her cheek, inhaling the scent of prey and pups. "Bera, my sweet, are you coming to war with me?"

She chuckles. "No, predator, you are coming to war with me."

I tsk. "We will do this my way or no way. We will spare as many of my males as we can. We will not slaughter and spill unnecessary blood. I will not rule as the Rai of ashes and bones."

Bera purses her lips.

Tash grunts and whips his tail, and Bera nods.

"One more thing. Whisper on the winds so that Mae can hear you. Tell her I'm coming."

CHAPTER TWENTY-ONE

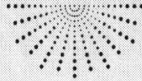

LENA

I no longer sit at the foot of the throne, but in Vor's place on the throne next to Dani, who's wearing a crown marking her as Raiyes of the Ra tribe. It's a massive crown fit for the large head of a male predator, but Dani wears it nevertheless, saddling me with the cute little tiara Vor has given me. Her eyes, the silver of her huntress, appear crazed this evening as another Ra male is sacrificed in the hall.

After Vor's death, Dani won't tell me what she did with Ark.

After Vor's death, Dani has sacrificed a Ra male each evening.

They pray for Aimea's favor, and Dani is convinced the brutal goddesses will grant her one. Doom, Dani says, is unavoidable, and we must purge the weak in order to rise stronger.

In my mind, Mae has gone quiet and so have the fires in the city. Most people have left either in pursuit of a warmer climate or in fear of Mae's wrath. They say she will strike with the vengeance of thousand suns and burn the city to the ground.

I doubt that.

Mae is sad.

I think she loved Ark with all my heart, and in a way, both Ark and I have failed her.

Next to me, Dani clears her throat, and a tear slides down her cheek. It must be a trick of the waning sunlight piercing the windows, for this female has no heart. Which is probably why she'll survive whatever comes next, and I won't. Or maybe I will if I embrace Mae and her power, and especially the power she holds over all the lies.

I may not have fire, but next to Dani, I always have lies.

The Sha-males circle the firepit relentlessly around the clock, trying and failing to give it life. They throw pleading glances my way, but I can't help them.

At twilight, the Ra armies sing in the streets. It is a greeting, a welcoming song for their goddess of twilight. When Dani brings Ark to the sacrificial dais, I wonder how his males will see him off, with silence or with a song.

I only know that people will miss him. Far more people will miss him than they do Vor, the male all but history for most people, even for his mother.

Dani takes my hand.

I will my body to heat up and burn her, but nothing happens. I want to lie. I want to outsmart her. I want her to trust me, believe me, lower her guard, and then I want to strike at her and set this horrible place on fire.

My thoughts scare me.

They excite me too, for Mae is me and I am her and I want her back. She gave me courage, even purpose to exist in this world and do some good for a change.

Dani's hand is soft and warm atop mine. She leans in and says, "They're expecting a public execution."

I swallow.

"And they will get one. Unless, of course, Mae gives us back the fire. If you do that, I will ensure Ark survives."

"Where is he?"

"In a hole where nobody will find him."

Those holes are terrible places. I've seen them on the outskirts of Tash's property. Deep holes the sizes of two wells, where predators put their enemies and leave them to rot. I need to get to Ark wherever he is, but Dani won't let me out of her sight. My new chambers are heavily guarded and without any portal access. Since my eyes are white like their eyes, enhancing my sight, I can now see their portals. They're beautiful golden lines bringing light into the dark spaces.

In the corner of the room, right under the painting of Mae rising out of the fire, the predators erected one such portal and enclosed it within a steel cage. I presume that's where they'll deliver Ark right before they execute him.

"Is it tonight? Will you bring him tonight?"

"Tomorrow at twilight."

"What do you want?" I grit out.

"Your firstborn." She speaks the truth. She won't feed me lies.

I place a hand on my belly. "I didn't know I was pregnant."

"You are. I smell it on you." Dani gets this dreamy look in her eyes. "My baby. He will be beautiful and all mine."

"All yours," I lie.

She eyes me, skeptical of my declaration.

"But first," I continue, "you have to swear to Bera you will spare Ark's life and mine and let us live out our lives somewhere in this world."

"I swear it," she lies, and it zaps my body as if I shot heroin into my veins. The power of lies is addictive, especially now, when nobody can light a fire and pray. Mae feeds off Dani's lies, and Dani has lived a life of lies. She's lied to both her mates, her children, her people. I only hope all her lies will eventually free us from her grip.

"I want to see Ark."

"Tonight?" she asks.

"Yes."

She motions for a male and whispers into his ear. The male leaves, and Dani says, "Do we have a deal?"

Good heavens, she lost her son and she has moved on as if nothing happened. "I'm curious, Dani, did you love Vor at all?"

Dani blinks, taken aback by my question. "He was my baby boy."

Is that a yes? Because Vor loved her.

"I know you're feeding off my lies, Mae, so I won't lie to you this time. It's too big a lie, too powerful." She leans in and whispers, "He was weak, and Ark did me a favor. Until your baby is ready to rule, I will rule the Ra lands. Mae will feed off my lies and thrive, and I will grow indispensable to her rule. She knows it even if you don't. And one span, she will grow bored of Ark and decide you are no longer a valuable vessel, and she will inhabit the one who will take care of her as one should take care of a goddess."

Truth. Dani speaks the truth. "You plan to take everything from me."

Dani smiles, a genuine smile, white eyes lifting at the corners. "No, stupid girl, I plan to give you everything."

"Give Mae everything, you mean."

Dani leans back in her seat. "Mae only wants the Ra crown."

That's not true. Mae wants Ark with all my heart, and Dani will never understand that. She believes Mae's separate from me, but we're not. We are one and the same, and so Mae feels what I feel. I know this like I know the alphabet.

"Bring him," Dani says.

The portal, a single golden line inside the large steel cage, expands on both ends and stands open enough for a single male to pass through. The hall falls silent as we await Ark's arrival. When he doesn't walk through the portal on his end, wherever that might be, Dani taps her claw.

Rising from the throne, I wait, my heart pounding. I don't know if I want him to come through or not. If he doesn't come through, it means he's dead on the other end, having not survived the wounds Dani inflicted on him. If he comes through the portal, it means he's doomed for either death or an imprisonment hunters can't survive. When I was at Tash's, males talked about the holes and said no hunter survives more than a cycle inside those prisons. The confined dark space makes hunters restless, and eventually, they go mad.

Ark's been gone more than a week.

The minutes tick by, and the space in the cage remains empty.

Dani takes my hand and rises. The predators part as we walk to the window. A Sha-male covered in a mourning robe and hood unlatches it and moves aside.

The Ra removed and cleared out all the market stalls to make room for hundreds of thousands of warriors. Some of the predators stand under the Ra flag, others under flags I don't recognize, but I know Dani wants me to see her army. She wants me to know what's at her disposal. Mae's disposal.

"All this is for us to command, Mae. Bera favors the fittest, and we are by far and wide the fittest, most powerful army in the tribal lands. There's never been a better time than now to invite Aimea and conquer."

"Conquer?"

"The tribal lands," Dani states, her eyes silver and wild with madness. "All the lands under a single Raiyes. United with all their goddesses paying tribute to you, for fire is a necessity of our life. We can't live without it. It is what you've always wanted, Mae, and I will be the female who gives it to you."

"Nah, bitch, I always wanted a stable home surrounded by people who love me and who I love back."

Dani shakes her head. "I see you still think like prey. I have much work to do yet."

Thick fog starts accumulating beyond the armies, and soon we can barely see the mountain ranges.

"What's happening?" I ask.

"Aimea," Dani shouts into the sky, which darkens instantly. "I call upon you to purify us and take the human spirits from the lands. They're prey and make us weak. Come to me, oh Aimea, and you shall rule over them all."

A shot of lies travels up my veins. Dani is lying to the goddess of doom. She won't allow Aimea to rule anything. She wants to use her for something, but not to rule.

The sky darkens so fast, it's as if a storm is coming, but there's no wind and no clouds. It's eerily quiet in the city filled with hundreds of thousands of warriors. It's the quiet before the storm, and I feel like I'm in the eye of the hurricane.

"Twilight," Dani whispers.

"Dani, please stop this madness."

"Aimea," she calls, and dark mist descends from the sky.

"No, no, no," I start backing away from the window. "Dani, you have to stop. You'll destroy everything!"

She grabs my hand and tugs me back. "That's the idea, dear. We have to wipe out the weak so we can unite and rise strong again."

Crinkling noises come from behind me, and I turn to see the main firepit in the Hall of Eternal Flame where Dani burned Vor's body flare, its flames reaching the ceiling, then separating and running down the walls. The sacred scrip-

tures the Sha wrote on the walls ignite and glow an irides-
cent blue. Bera's painting of all the goddesses starts melting.
The predators inside murmur and push away from the walls.

"Get out of here," I tell them as my body heats up, as Mae
starts rebelling against the presence of the goddess of doom.

The predators stay indoors.

Dani chuckles. "I knew you'd agree with me, Mae. Go on,
my dearest, burn it all to the ground." The crazy female takes
my cheeks between her hands and keeps them there even
when my skin heats up her palms. Dani's skin sizzles, and she
smiles, the silver eyes of her huntress watching me, threatening me. "Spread your wings, Mae. Wild like the fire, free as
a bird, burn through the weak, for the strong will find a way
to survive."

A drop of rain lands on the window. Another and
another, and soon it's pouring, with thunder striking down
on the roofs.

"Your daughter, Aoa, is here," Dani says. "Thunder and
pain. She can feel your power even across the lands."

The window swings open, and Dani and I both jump
away. Wind gushes inside and propels the fire upward
toward the ceiling, melting all the beautiful paintings that
I've been told have been here since the beginning of these
people's times.

Dani sniffs, and I look over. Blood trails out of her nose.
She swipes it with a thumb and marks her cheek with a red
streak. "Eme!" she shouts. "Where are you, Eme? Show yourself on this span."

The fog beyond the armies in the city clears, and another
army appears, this one smaller, maybe a few hundred males,
but mighty because Bera has come. Imani wears a golden
wrap over her curly hair and matching golden armor. Above
her, birds of prey circle, their blue feathers flashing like stars
in the night.

I look at Dani's profile. Her nose won't stop bleeding, and even the Sha who has stood like a dark, ominous presence next to us sniffs. I presume he's bleeding as well.

Bera lifts an arm.

The predators start chanting her war song, banging their weapons against the shields. The winds gush through the city, lifting everything in their path. The flags wave as if saying goodbye. The rain pours over the fires breaking out in the city while thunder strikes the palace's roof making me jumpy as if Aoa might actually strike me next. She might. She and Mae didn't part on the best terms.

"Talk to Bera," Dani says and moves to stand behind me. The cold edge of a blade touches my throat, and Dani grips my hair and yanks my head back. "Bera," Dani shouts, "if you pit your predators against me, I will make a meal of your pet!"

A chuckle carries on the winds, and Bera lifts two fingers.

The small army she brought charges. The birds of prey descend.

The Sha-male steps forward and places a dagger in my hand.

"Back off Sha," Dani hisses and nicks my neck.

Bera is the goddess of war. Stories I've heard over the fire say whoever Bera stands for always wins, and Bera stands with Mae. Maybe that's why I always thought of Imani as the mother I never had. She comforted me in the darkest of times, when I thought I'd finally crack and hurt myself on purpose so I didn't have to suffer anymore.

I grip the dagger the Sha gave me and know I'll only get one chance at this.

Dani has me by the hair, and she's dragging me across the room. The fire from the walls forms a trail and follows me, catching the Sha-male's robe on fire. The robe burns, but the

Sha makes no noise as he calmly takes long strides to follow me.

"Stand back, Sha-male," Dani's shouting at my ear and moving backward. The male, now engulfed in fire, keeps walking toward us, and as his clothes burn away, he pulls back his hood. The second I see his face, I burst into flames, flooding the hall with fire.

The explosion shakes the palace, and the ground under us splits. And yet, I touch his face as if we're the only people in the room and as if nothing is happening around us.

"Ark," I whisper. "What are you doing here?"

"Came to collect my prize. You miss me?"

Fully aware that my body and everything around us is on fire, I throw my arms around his neck. Ark doesn't burn. Mae's fire can't touch him, and I couldn't be happier, because this place is going to burn to ashes, and he and I will be the only two left standing.

"Lena." He kisses me. "Pull back the fire."

"I don't know how," I say as people scream.

Ark snaps his gaze up and past me, and I turn just before Dani slips into her chambers. Bright golden portal light illuminates the seams around the door.

"She won't get very far," he says. "Mas is controlling all the portals in and out of Ralna. There's no escaping the city." Ark looks around him, then grabs my hand and tugs. We run toward the windows, which are packed with males jumping out of the palace. We're almost there, just a few more steps. A pillar starts falling, and I freeze, unable to move from under it, my entire life flashing before my eyes.

My sister's retreating face plastered to the window of a red pickup truck as the family who took her in for foster care drives off, leaving me behind. They separated us, and there was nothing we could do about it.

The moment when the captain of the cruiser announced we

were all gonna die.

Ark snarling at me when I peed my pants the first time I saw his canines. He accused me of marking his ship and was a total asshole about it, locked me up for days as punishment.

The night we spent together in his furs, where he held me, whispering prayers into my ear. I felt safe and at home, and I wanted to spend a lifetime wrapped up in Ark.

Ark sweeps me into his arms now, and a pillar crashes, shaking the ground under us, raising dust everywhere. Dirt covers our faces, and I cough as he moves into a corner, still carrying me like a bride. Some couple we make.

I wipe the dust away from my eyes, and he sneezes several times until the debris settles and we can see again. Ark approaches the window, and because I'm on fire, males clear out of the way. He hops onto the sill and looks down. "Be ready in three. One…"

Flames are rising out of my body, and anywhere I go, anywhere he takes me, is bound to burn to ashes. "Ark, I love the palace," I tell him. "It feels like home to me, and I've never had this feeling before. I love this city with the big market that needs expanding. I love that my sister crash-landed with me and we met some amazing people and we found acceptance and love, and maybe we are all crazy"—I put my hand up before Ark starts chanting Amti's name three times to ward off the madness—"what with goddesses inside us and all, but we are still women, and our biggest strength is creation, not destruction. I want to save the palace and the predators from burning. I won't let Mae burn it down. She will stop, or she can go find someone else to carry her load."

Ark has a strange expression.

"What is it?" I ask him.

"I love you, Lena."

Leave it to Ark to drop the *I love you* bomb in the middle of chaos. "I love you too."

CHAPTER TWENTY-TWO

ARK

*T*he pressure that started accumulating inside my chest since I woke up at Hart's leaves me as I utter those three words I've dreaded saying to a female ever since I was a wee boy. The first woman I ever said that to was my mother, who reprimanded me for it, told me a female would use them against me, and to never repeat them again.

But Lena is kind of heart, fierce of mind, and wild of a spirit that's destroying the city I intend to rule. I'd always wanted peace and prosperity for my tribe, and I figured the best way to do that was to stop warring all the time and on all fronts. North. South. West. Hell, if we had gills, we'd dive into the ocean and start a war with the sea creatures. It's in our blood.

Creation is also in our blood, or the seed, actually, and mine is growing inside her. I can't compromise her and my pup and choose the palace over them. I'll build her another palace.

The second pillar collapses, and the roof is about to fold. "Three," I tell her and jump out the window with her. Her scream follows us all the way down until we hit the water, my body shielding hers from the impact, my legs instantly bruising from the fall. Under the water, I expect Lena to start panicking and scrambling, clawing at me with blunt nails, but she doesn't.

Her fire is extinguished, and as we sink, she looks at me with flames dancing in her white eyes.

I kiss her and propel us upward. I don't let her breathe when we emerge because she tastes of prey and firelight, and she is mine.

"Don't mind us bleeding over here!" Hart's voice breaks the moment.

Hart's on the shore, at Jal's former stand's location, battling seven members of the Eten tribe, which my mother formed an alliance with. The rest of Eten's are pushing a massive stone thrower down the marketplace street, toward the palace. They're gonna destroy the concrete pillars we use as memorials for our fallen tribemates. They'll collapse the palace.

There has never been a better time to conquer the Ra tribe, and they're coming for us. Finally, division will kill us. We, the Ra, don't need external enemies. We will kill ourselves all on our own. If those were Ra males wanting to destroy the palace, I'd probably help them. But these are not Ra males (or Ka, for that matter) and I don't take kindly to others pissing on my turf.

Besides, Lena expressed love for the palace, the wretched fucking place I grew up in and want to tear down, so now I changed my mind. Won't destroy the place. Maybe with her and my pups running around in there, the place will change, become the home it once was while my father was still alive.

I swim with Mae toward Hart, surveying the marketplace for some of my tribemates who are on my side. Climbing the shore, I spot a few of my males, but none fit enough to secure

Lena's safe passage to Bera up on the hillside and away from mayhem.

"Looking for someone?" A male sneaks up behind me.

I spin and slash.

He bends his body backward and escapes the slice of my sharp ax. A piece of blond braid falls on the ground.

It's Mas, Ka portal master, and I almost beheaded him.

"What's the matter, Ark. A little on edge lately?"

"Fuck you, Ka. You here to open the portals? Report on my mother? Or have you a death wish?" I gesture with my ax at his hair on the ground, half the braid at least. Holy Herea, that makes me all warm and happy.

He smirks. "You lost your mommy?" Extending a hand, he offers it to Lena while his other hand flies through the air. Lo and behold, the little Ka bitch has had a secret portal right beside Jal's stand this entire time. Makes me want to take my blade to his entire head and shave off all his hair. Won't be so pretty after that.

Registering my shock, he winks. "Don't go killer on me. I'll collapse it for good… If you win."

"How's the win looking so far?"

"Not good." He stares pointedly at me. "We could use another skilled ax in the field."

"Are you saying I'm skilled?" I nudge Lena toward him and note her resistance. I nod at Mas to take her by force. I can't fight Bera's war if I'm worrying about someone killing my marked goddess.

"I am saying the Etens have taken advantage of Bera's presence and will wage a war for land. Maybe she'll start favoring them."

I kiss Lena on the forehead and push her away. Mas grabs her, and her screaming protests hurt my chest, that awkward weight settling in the middle of my rib cage again. The two disappear as if they were never there, and I snap my head up to see them materialize right behind Bera on the hill. Bera's standing on her own two feet, which means my brother is somewhere around here.

"Tash!" I shout, then clap Hart on the ass as I walk by him. "Nice form. Keep it up."

"Excuse me while I bleed for your future," he throws after me with a grunt when the male he's fighting likely stabs him somewhere.

He's bleeding for his future too, but I don't have time for Hart's theatrics as the legion of Etens keep pushing the stone thrower. They're inside the market square Lena enjoys so much, and it fucking lights my fire that they're destroying the stands and small flower shops that give this place feminine charms.

There's a flash of blue in the sky above the stone-throwing machine, and I grab my second ax. I don't trust the Om birds. One bird releases his claws, and a male drops, landing on top of the machine, slicing and killing the Etens. He's so covered in paint and blood that it takes me a moment to recognize him.

It's my brother Tash, and he's drawing attention to himself. The Etens walking alongside the machine climb the thrower to get to him.

"Tash," I shout again, but I doubt he can hear me. Bera runs strong within him, and all Tash knows now is a drive to eliminate the enemy, which is all fine and great, but I know how Tash is in battle, and I dislike when my brother fights without me. He's prone to heroism and other dumb shit that gets a male killed.

I stop at the end of the square, a few steps from the water, and wait. A group of three Etens see me and rush toward me, and I smile as the wind blows past me, carrying Bera's whisper: "Rai."

The Etens attack in a flurry of hands wielding a total of

three axes and two swords. I duck, roll, and turn up behind them, slicing across their spines before they can pivot. Blood spurts across my lips, and I lick it, growling at the pleasant taste.

"Ark," Tash shouts. "Get out of the way."

I turn toward the machine. Tash is at the top, bodies all around him.

"No can do. Stop the thrower."

"No can do. Don't know how. This thing is gonna hit the pillars. The palace will fall. Do something, Ark!"

If the machine hits the pillars, it'll topple the palace.

"We have to stop the thrower," Hart says. Nar joins him, heaving breaths, holding his side, limping on one leg. Hart's assessing his brother and orders him to stand down and move away, but of course, he stays next to Hart.

Mas pops in and assumes a battle stance. Seeing the machine rolling toward us and yet no enemies, he scratches his head. "What are we doing?"

"I'm ideating on how to stop the thrower from hitting the pillars."

"Let me know when you come up with something," he says.

The four of us stand there, willing the machine that's the size of three houses to stop rolling down the square. Tash is up there doing goddess knows what, but he got the machine to at least slow down if not stop.

He waves from above. "Get out of the way!"

I'm not leaving. This palace is a symbol of the strength of my tribe, and Lena loves it and wouldn't let Mae burn it down. I can't stand by and let the Etens take it down. It would kill something inside me to watch it fall into the water.

Pride. It would kill my pride, and pride is often all that's kept me alive, because it sure as fuck wasn't motherly love and support.

I charge the stone thrower like it's a living predator. Hands on the machine's front, I push back, roaring when the wood makes contact with my body, my boots scraping the cobblestone as the machine keeps moving. Hart joins me, and our faces are plastered to the wood as we push, trying to stop it with sheer strength. His face is bright red as he strains his bulky form, biceps the size of my head. This motherfucker is fit.

Nar and Mas join in, and I hear boots behind me, then next to me. Sniffing, I recognize Kore's feminine scent.

"Hey, boys," she says, then groans as she settles in at my right, hands out and pushing.

"You shouldn't be straining yourself." Tash comes around and starts pushing next to her.

"What are you, my wet nurse?" Kore says.

I chuckle. Even if Kore is pregnant and he's right, he knows better than to talk shit like this to our sister.

We push and get the machine to slow, but the downhill trajectory only means the machine will gain momentum. Either it's gonna run us over or we're gonna stop it in the next three steps. A screech announces a bird of prey before the wind he creates with his wings hits us.

"Not helping," I grit out and continue straining.

Hart's so red in the face, he's about to burst.

Kore's screaming in my ears as she tries to push harder.

Tash is breathing hard.

The winds from the Om batter us and knock us all into the water.

Snarling, we look up as the biggest motherfucking Om I've ever seen has his claws on the machine, batting his huge wings backward, trying to lift it.

"A case of gold says the Om will lift it," Mas says.

"I accept," Nar says.

The machine lifts a bit, then drops, and the Om screeches.

"Uh-oh," Nar says. "A case of gold."

"He's just testing the weight," Mas replies.

"Ark," Tash nudges me.

I throw my arms around him and pat him on the back. "Thank you, brother."

"Don't thank me yet. Mother intends to kill you still."

I step back and follow his gaze past the machine the Om is starting to lift and remove. The market is full of Ra warriors. Standing in the front is my mother in full battle armor. She wears white on white and the silver fur of my dead father over her double swords. Those are for show. Mother is an archer.

"Let me do it, Ark," Kore spats. "Let me end her."

We're outnumbered at least fifty to one, and the odds of dying are great. Jokes aside, I'm not suicidal, and especially not now when I have a Raiyes with a pup on the way to look forward to. I worry about Tash, though. I'm always fucking worrying he'll overprotect me even when he knows I can take care of myself.

"Tash, you wanna sit this out?" I whisper.

Nar snorts. "I was thinking the same thing about Hart."

"You boys are cute," Kore says and steps forward. "Mother, surrender now, and the Rai will spare your life."

"I see no Rai among you, and the Ka have no say in our land."

Her army shouts and spits insults, and I stand embarrassed. Once upon a time, I did that too. I insulted the Ka tribe, which isn't so different from us after all. We are members of the same clan, same ancestry. It's just that Hart and I could never live under the same rule, neither mine nor his, so we will not unite under one tribe, but we will unite the tribes and live in peace as neighbors.

Casually, as if I care not about Mother's threat, I throw a hand over Kore's shoulder. "Yield, Mother, and I will spare the lives of your entire army." Provided they kneel for me, of course, but I'll go about that later.

Her males laugh. If I were in their place, I'd have laughed as well. Six predators against an army is hardly a bother for the army to dispatch.

"Bera," I whisper, "you still with me, girl?"

Fire encircles the square. The army spooks and forms tighter ranks.

"Hold position," Mother shouts. "Fire is the essence of our life. We do not fear it. Mae will favor the winner. Bera will favor the strong."

"Tash," Nar whispers. "Bera is still with us, no?"

Tash smirks. "What's the matter, Ka? You need a pregnant human to boost your morale?"

"Fuck you, Ra."

"I did and made two. What have you got to show for it?"

Lightning slices the sky, and Nar looks up. "Next one will fry you, Tash."

I spin and bark, "Silence!" Measuring dicks can wait. I glance at Hart. As per usual, he's quieter than most males, mentally preparing for the kill. A small nod at me tells me he's ready. I swipe two fingers over the red paint on my face, lift them, and look up the hill where the goddesses who walk the lands have gathered.

We're at the bottom, in the water, and in a terrible position altogether when Bera whistles, calling for the end, calling for slaughter, calling for one winner at the cost of all. Mother screams her battle cry, eager to kill me and win.

CHAPTER TWENTY-THREE

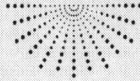

ARK

*T*he initial clash of the armies is always the hardest. One never knows which male is gunning for you or how many or from where the sharp edge of a blade will strike.

Four males run for me, bringing down their axes. I skip and dance around them, appear behind their backs, and slice two. One falls dead, the other wounded; the other two males charge again. There's just enough room between their bodies to kneel, and so I do. I kneel and stick out my axes and gut them.

Impaled, they bend over the axes, and rising, I rip out their bellies.

Moving on, I wipe my face and rush into the fray, where the three Ka males fight the majority of the army. I slice the enemy from behind as I make my way inside the mayhem so I can fight alongside Hart and see what that's like for a change. And I almost make it inside when he glances toward me, and his eyes widen.

I spin and catch the arrow aimed at my back. My mother is running, her skirts telling me which way she went. I sprint after her and find her on the edge of the battlefield. She turns and aims at me, then looses the arrow.

I dodge, snatching the arrow in midair.

She looses again.

I dodge closer yet.

I grab the back of her head and bring her to me, piercing her cold heart with her arrow that I caught. Mother gasps and drops her bow, then grips my shoulders, her body bending backward. I keep her upright and yank her by the hair so I can watch the life be extinguished from her eyes. Silver huntress eyes watch me as blood trickles out of the corner of her mouth. I lick it, taste, and spit out the poison she intended for me.

It spreads quickly, effectively making her bleed pale pink then white as the poison destroys her from the inside out, rupturing her blood cells. The huntress's silver eyes dim.

"I will see you on the other side," she says.

"Save me a seat at the throne."

My mother looks up as the clouds clear for the moon's bright light. It illuminates her dead face, and I lay her down, leaving the arrow in her chest. A wall of fire rages behind me, and the males that saw us now stand idle, confused, lost, not knowing what to do. Several of them try running, but the fire wall can't be breached by anyone but Mae and me.

The fighting is dying down, the skies are clearing. The birds of prey ascend and circle above us.

Eyes on our mother, Tash limps over, a deep gash marring his thigh, but that doesn't stop him from being the first male who kneels and kisses my ring. Behind me, I feel a powerful presence as the fire continues to rage, making us all sweat, threatening anyone who dares to question Mae's choice of a partner. But the scent of prey gives her away immediately.

"Join me," I say and extend a hand. Lena clasps it and

squeezes, but stares straight at the army, showing no emotions, even though I can smell her turmoil. She stares at them the way a goddess would, daring them not to fall in line behind Tash.

"Rai," Bera whispers on the wind.

I whistle.

And the Ra males kneel.

CHAPTER TWENTY-FOUR

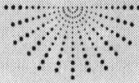

LENA

*M*y first wedding fantasy came about the night after a boy in high school kissed me. I remember because it's one of the happiest memories of my life. I lay in the attic on a throwaway single bed and imagined a small event attended by a few people, mainly from his side of the family because I didn't have anyone besides Amanda on mine.

But it was a lovely imaginary event where I married a handsome man who was in love with me. I wore a pretty white dress that trailed behind me as I walked down the aisle. There were white roses everywhere.

As I grew older, the vision of a perfect wedding didn't change for me. Even when the odds weren't in my favor, I guess I never stopped wishing for a better life.

However, never in my wildest fantasies did I imagine not marrying at all.

And I certainly did not imagine I would become a queen of a tribe on a faraway planet nobody on Earth even knows about. But God works in mysterious ways.

And so do the goddesses.

Inside me, Mae is no longer another person, but an extension of my consciousness. Her emotions and mine are in sync as our spirits mingle and make peace with each other.

Ark is our link, the male who brought her and me together as he's brought together his tribe and offered them a better life of prosperity and peace with their neighbors.

In Ralna, tribemates stand shoulder to shoulder holding lit candles and torches as my raft drifts toward the belly of the palace, where soldiers will receive me and portal me into the Hall of the Eternal Flame.

Predators see in the dark, so they don't need fire to light the path, and neither do I anymore since Ark marked me and my eyes adjusted to living on Nomra Prime.

The people light candles and torches as a connection to me, and that makes me sit up straighter in the raft, the energy from their prayer making my body buzz with happiness.

A little girl, maybe seven years old, catches my attention. She's dyed her hair red and wears it brushed straight down like mine. She shows me her hand and wiggles her fingers. Her claws are filed and painted pink. I wave back, wondering if my baby girl will look like me or her father.

Oh God, Ark is up there, waiting for me to assume the throne with this formal ceremony. Thinking about assuming the throne makes my palms sweat, and I slip on the white gloves he gave me after he lost day one of the games.

He lost day two of the games as well.

He has lost a lot to gain his rule, namely both parents and a childhood, as well as most of his young adulthood. But he persevered. He persevered against the odds with a strong sense of faith in himself and what he would become. We could all use some faith in ourselves.

At the portal that leads from the water up to the palace, the soldiers, dressed in shiny polished new iertos, open the portal that leads into the hallway just before the main hall. The portal gap grows larger so I can see the entire hallway and those standing there.

It's just Tash and Bera. Disappointment at not seeing my sister crashes over me, but as Dani taught me, I show no emotion. If they read disappointment or displeasure on my face, they might misinterpret the sentiment and think it's aimed at them, when I couldn't be happier that Imani and I are now related. Officially, she's my sister-in-law.

I can say what I will about Dani, but I can't deny she was a formidable female with the self-control of a rock. Reserving my emotional outbursts or having people see how I feel will help me when I assume that throne, and it has helped me control some of Mae's fire. I practice controlling fire every day. It has become my mission to wield fire and use it for good.

Imani smiles as I approach her, my chest filled with the flutters of butterfly wings as I hear chatter inside the palace's main hall and behind the massive closed doors. It reminds me again of the first day in a new school.

And…I'm gonna vomit. No, no. I shake my head. I'm fine. It'll be fine. "How many people made it for the ceremony?" I manage to ask.

"The hall is packed," Imani says.

"But it fits seven thousand."

"It too needs expansion?" Tash says and raises an eyebrow. He coordinated the marketplace expansion effort, and construction has already started.

"The hall can remain as it is for now," I say.

Tash smiles, bowing his head slightly. "Yes, Raiyes."

"Wall to freshly painted wall of predators at your service," Imani says. When the workers came, the first thing Ark ordered repaired was the fire damage on the wall Bera had painted.

Two days later, the workers already started, and Imani and Tash visited. Bera picked up her brush like she would pick up a sword, and lo and behold, the work on the restoration took only a few nights, those tribal members working overtime to leave her with a huge white canvas.

Tash and Bera stayed for the rest of the winter, and now into spring, with Imani painting the entire city.

She bends and whispers at my ear in the tongue Mae and Bera speak most often, the ancient language that sounds like a siren song from Bera's seductive lips. "All the tribes from all the lands have come to witness Mae assume her throne. Some are not Ra friends. Keep that in mind."

I nod.

"Are you ready?" Tash presses a palm against the door and pushes it open, not waiting for my reply. Ready as I'll ever be!

I step into a dark space. Not even the portals are lit. Confused, I frown.

"Ark said a show of power wouldn't hurt," Bera whispers from behind me.

Tash slides up next to me and offers me his elbow. "The enemies are always watching," he says under his breath.

I slide my hand under his arm as one would at a wedding, and Tash walks me "down the aisle." With a thought, I light the torches one by one, and as we walk, a trail of flames follows behind us. The Sha-males gathered around the seven firepits jump back when the flames ignite, every one of them reaching the ceiling.

The people outside start chanting prayers loudly as I approach Ark, who is standing before his throne, looking… nervous. But that's not possible. Ark's never nervous, so I must be misreading his expression. Besides, he rarely shows his real emotions in public. Dani was his mother, after all.

Tash stops at the steps, and I climb to reach Ark. The silver eyes of his hunter are watching me. He grips my waist and brings me flush against his body, purring low in his throat. Oh, he's just horny. The weight of his heavy cock rests on my growing belly.

"A white dress?" he asks.

"I fancy myself a bride."

Ark threads locks of my hair between his claws. Against my belly, his cock jerks, and my pussy starts throbbing. Ark sniffs at the same time Tash takes a few steps away from the throne. The entire hall smells my arousal. It's something I'm gonna get used to, I guess.

"You look beautiful," Ark says and runs his claws through my hair again. He brings a lock to his nose and inhales, then starts purring loudly.

Ark's display of affection makes me flush. He can still make me blush like a virgin, even though the things he's done to me in the furs are something I'd never even tell my sister. Thumb brushing my hip, he tucks one side of my hair behind my ear and takes my hand in his, his silver eyes captivating me, pounding me with his dominance, promising me everything I could ever dream of and things I can't.

"Thank you, Ark."

"For?"

"Never giving up on me."

Ark slips something onto my finger, then, holding out my hand, he drops to one knee. There's a golden band holding up a giant red stone erected on a golden mound on my finger. It matches Ark's more modest Rai ring.

He kisses my ring, then stands and offers me the throne.

Still staring at the beautiful ring and how the flames in the room reflect off it, I sit down and swallow. "This is the prettiest thing anyone has ever given me."

"Prettier than all the things Vor and Dani gave you?"

I look up and chuckle. "Yes." He's so competitive. Smiling, I take stock of the room and the lovely people gathered there.

Right in front of me sits my sister. When her white eyes lock with mine, tears gather immediately, and I struggle to control the outburst of joy, then decide not to give a fuck about emotions right now and rush down the steps to hug her. She feels warm and familiar, and I missed her.

"I told you he'd be their king," she says and kisses my cheek. "And you lied about how you felt about him."

"I did."

"Goddess of lies," she says. "And my queen." Amanda wipes the runny makeup under her eyes. "They wouldn't let me come and see you. Said Dani would use me, hurt me and the baby. Ark hid us in butt-fucking nowhere land, didn't let us come to the city until later in the night, or I'd have come for your games, sister. I'd have come."

"Oh, that's okay." Ark hid her so nobody would have leverage in the games. Or over me. My chin quivers.

Amanda smiles. "I'm so proud of you. Don't cry. All that nice makeup is gonna run like mine."

I squeal, hug my sister, and try not to cry and ruin the makeup a team of Ra females did for me. They spent hours dressing me up and making me look this way for today. And to their credit, I've never looked as pretty as I do now. Amanda and I part, and I sit back down on the throne, where Ark places his heavy hand on top of mine.

Technically, today isn't my wedding day, but I asked for a white dress, a hall that's decorated with flowers, my sister, and a bunch of people who love me and who I love back, especially that one handsome predator sitting beside me on the throne.

"This is the happiest day of my life," I say.

EPILOGUE

Ten Turns Later
Ark

Turns ago, before I met my Raiyes, if someone had told me that portals between Ralna and Kalia would reopen again, I'd have told them that I already knew they would and thanked them politely for the reassurance I never needed when I set out to make peace with Hart.

If someone told me I would capture the attention of a goddess who wields fire and lies, I'd have told them that if Mae roamed the lands again, I know she'd land on my dick. I am the fittest of the Ra, and she's the Ra goddess.

But one thing I couldn't have planned for is my Raiyes. I did not account for the human capturing my heart and stealing my soul and making me mate her and give her pups. We have four pups. Four. All are female, including the twins born in between my youngest and my oldest, who prefer running around in huntress instead of on their two legs.

Tash calls the twins the Arkies.

I think it's cute.

My Raiyes thinks it sounds like a pair of Yorkies. When she described what a Yorkie is, a small animal that likes to cuddle in people's laps and look pretty, I don't see much of a difference. My girls like it when I pet them, and they especially like to hunt terriks with me, something I hear a terrier-type dog was originally bred for. Hunting.

I place Esna and Naye on the floor and stand to stretch the back muscle I pulled running after them this very morning. The girls trail after Kore, wagging their tails because their aunt Kore is taking them on vacation to the Blood Dunes where they get to bathe in the sun during the winter cycles while the rest of us are freezing.

Good ol' Eme still bleeds any predators who step onto her sands, so I'm staying where I am, in Ralna with my Raiyes, who should be ready to leave by now. She isn't because she rarely is ready to leave on time.

The portal leading into our quarters at the top of the palace opens, and I step through it and into our living space, where the painting of Bera nursing a wee Mae greets me. I whisper a prayer to Bera's fine tits so that she may hear me and know I haven't forgotten to pray to her lest she think I've grown ungrateful for the blessings she bestowed upon me. I'm the only predator with four female children.

Sniffing, I sense my Raiyes at her armoire, and staying close to the shadows, I stalk her, the scent of prey always and forever calling me to both ravage and fuck her.

Raiyes wears a red Om fur over her shoulders, a little white miniskirt, and black thigh-high boots. On top of her red hair rests a crown made of golden flames. Females who make an art of painting faces come to the palace begging to paint my Raiyes, and her makeup is always the finest in the lands.

Even without all the glamour her status affords her, she's beautiful because of the goodness that shines from inside.

Lena catches my reflection in the mirror and screams.

I place a palm over her mouth and bring her flush to my body, lifting her little fuck-me miniskirt in the process. Under it, my Raiyes wears nothing, and I trail my claw over the back of her thigh, reach the knee, and force it to bend. I lift her leg and place it on the armoire so I have better access to her pussy.

I stroke it, making her wet while she watches me in the mirror.

"You're late again," I say, and bite her neck while I unsnap my ierto and take out my cock. I enter her wet pussy in a single thrust, then grab her jaw and turn her head a bit so I can watch flames dance in her eyes. "You are most beautiful when I fuck you."

Lena smiles, a blush spreading over her cheeks. This is what I love the most about her. This humanity and the fact that turns later, I can still make her blush.

"Let's make fire, Rai."

"Let's." The torches ignite as I fuck her, and when I spill inside her, the fire on the roof roars, flames giving the impression that they'll touch the sky. Mae does like her power and showing it often, for the Ralna marketplace is the center of trade in our lands, and one never knows if someone might start thinking of conquering us. Making friends with the Ka means tribes from other places can portal in and out of the market with ease. Mae's fire reminds them who rules the Ra.

I tuck my wet cock inside my ierto and fix my weapons. Raiyes turns and beams up at me. Freshly fucked Raiyes is a sight to behold. Flecks of fire linger in her eyes like embers.

"I'm ready," she says.

"Thank Herea," I deadpan. "I was beginning to think I'd die an old lady-in-waiting."

"Asshole."

I wink. I am an asshole, and I'm lucky she puts up with me.

Lena slips on the white gloves she's worn for over ten winters now. I'm half tempted to burn them, for they're too old, and people are starting to talk, saying my Raiyes has only one pair of gloves. Over the turns I've bought her many more gloves, much better and much nicer than these. Her sister even knitted her several pairs, but no, during winter, Lena wears those old ones, and now she slips past me, pauses, then turns.

The air in the room changes, and I start itching everywhere. Mae is with me, and after all these turns I'm still not entirely comfortable when the goddess wants to address me like this. Fire spreads over the walls, and she speaks in an ancient tongue.

"I like them." She shows me her palms, indicating the gloves. "They tell the human she is loved and keep me humble." The flames die out, and Lena smiles. "They keep a goddess humble. I think I'll buy you a pair."

With that, she steps into the portal and stops in the market square, a big smile on her face. "By the way, Bera said you can have a boy next."

I join her and whisper. "I'm gonna have another child?" A male child. "Bera fucking loves me."

"Humble, Rai, humble."

"Humble can bend the knee," I hiss. "I'm the Rai with four daughters and a blazing-hot goddess of fire."

Lena waves at the crowds the army keeps at bay as we make our way to the opening of Amti's restaurant in Ralna, my brother Tash waiting for us at the door, wearing a bored expression. "Bera does not love you, Ark."

"She fucking does. I'm having another child, a male this time, but don't worry, I'm feeling real humble right now."

"Lies," Lena says. "Tell me more lies."

Inwardly celebrating the birth of my boy in the future, I grab Tash's head and kiss him on the cheek. He hates when I do that, and I like that I piss him off. In fact, I'm in a mood and feel like pissing everyone off, especially Hart. Where is he?

I scan the massive restaurant where Amti intends to feed my people her barbeque meat of questionable origin and find Hart's mane of dark hair between the blondie and the Omi.

I squeeze between mountains of muscle made of Hart and Omi, shake out my shoulders, and clear my throat. "Sorry I'm late," I lie.

Hart is holding a stick with chunks of flesh impaled on it over the fire. The meat sizzles, and my mouth waters as he pours something over it. The aroma alone makes most males standing around the firepit growl with hunger.

"What is the sauce made of?" Omi asks.

"It's a glaze. Terrik blood cooked with Bera's nectar."

I eye his stick and lick my teeth, and just as he's about to take a bite, I snatch the stick from him and rip off the biggest chunk of meat. I chew on the food, which has the most exquisite sweet taste. It melts on my tongue. My eyes roll to the back of my head. "Herea's holy pussy," I say and proceed to eat Hart's meal.

"Some spans," Hart says, "I sit happily by my pond thinking about making a coat out of you, Ark."

I pick off a piece of meat and offer to feed it to him the way I feed my youngest pup. He swats my arm away.

"Some things never change," I retort. "The Ra take from Ka, and the Ka whine about it."

"Until his handsome son steals one of our daughters," Lena says.

I choke, and the Raiyes stands next to me so she can pat me on the back.

Hart's son is holding her hand, and my Raiyes takes the stick I stole from his father and gives it to the boy. The boy has dark hair and clear chiseled lines on his face. It also doesn't help he's twice the size of other males his age, with the playful smile of his mother and not the brooding, domineering nature of his father. I recognize trouble when I see it.

"Raiyes," I hiss, "why would you say something like that?"

Lena shrugs. "He came up to me to ask when we will hold Poya's games."

Everyone thinks that's funny and cute. I do not. Nope.

"Hart, if your boy comes near Poya, I'd start a war over that." Nobody takes my girls. They will never have games. Non-bleeding virgins forever and ever. I shudder.

Hart's laughing so hard, he barely manages to speak. "Why do you think Bera gave you four girls?"

"To start wars over them, of course." I'm gonna kill him and start one now.

Bera's seductive laughter spreads through the place. "You Ra, always with your wars."

"Mmhm." I nod at Hart. "It'll be your fault."

Hart laughs harder.

Lena slips her gloved hand into mine and lifts my hand to her lips. She kisses my ring.

"Long live the peace between the Ka and Ra."

When I don't respond, the fire flares.

We all take a cautious step back. "Long live the peace," Hart and I say in unison.

∾

Twenty turns later, the Ka heir won Poya's games. Ka and Ra blood shall mix, uniting the tribes once again.

. . .

***

Hi, Milana here, and I hope your day is going well. I'm on my bed in my pajamas writing this note to you as I prepare Arked for departure into readerdome.

The moment Ark popped up in the Hall during Stephanie's games in book 1, I knew he was gonna be trouble. The way he came on the page, I knew the asshole's gonna close the series. And so he did, the Tribes series ended with Ark's book. Can you believe it's been six books?

Le sigh. It's always hard for me to part from characters I've spent a year or more with and that's especially true for this big Tribes world that could probably bring in more stories in Milanaverse.

The way I see it tho, is I get to revisit Tribes every time a new reader comes into this world and writes me an email about it. It really is about how well I deliver what I promise to deliver and how that aligns with what you're looking for when you read. In the end, that alignment of what I write and what you want is what matters most. Well, at least to me.

So in all, I hope Arked delivered a story about a dominant fun yet loving monster who falls in love with a girl and tries not to die in the process. I also hope you enjoyed the world itself and that spending time inside this world took you away from the daily grind.

An Alpha romance is what you'll get from all my books: Dark world. Dominant Monster. Sassy heroine. High heat. And I have another story with those core elements coming just for you. It is a fast-paced high fantasy with high heat. Read the opening on the next page…

SAVAGE IN THE TOUCH

TEASER UPPR

*S*even houses hardly even counts as a village, but since our tavern, which also serves as a bed and breakfast, is the last stop before the mountain that travelers must scale on their journey to the capital city of Lyan, we get busy.

The inn is strategically located right at the exit to the valley, and we made sure we put up a sign that says: *No fluffy bed or pillows for another two moons.* Sixty spans is a long time to spend in the forested mountain living in tents. Not to mention, one never knows what kind of criminals lurk in the bushes and what kind of trouble awaits in the mountains.

The road to Lyan is paved with dangers.

Yet that doesn't stop the refugees passing through our little village. They escaped the horde that's been plowing through the south of the kingdom. They say the horde devours everything in its path. They say its hunger can't be tamed.

They say it's coming.

It's all a myth. The "horde" is nothing more than a gang of rebels, or at most our southern fae neighbors looking for

177

trouble. And trouble they shall find, since half a moon ago, the king's army passed through the village on their way south. This means they must have already reached and defeated the horde and are on their way back now.

"Hey, Mag." I greet my sister as I tap my fingernails on the bar, reminding the drunk in front of me to pay up and call it a night. The man isn't chatty, and the ominous threadbare black cloak he wears obscures most of his face, which gives me an impression he came in to drown his sorrows undisturbed. Here's to hoping I won't have to carry his ass up the stairs to the third floor.

Although, if I have to, I will. Third-floor room and board runs at eleven silvers, so a little extra leg work for the guy is included in the price.

"Hey," my sister says and dumps a large bag of potatoes at my feet. "Here you go." She wipes her hands on a dirty white apron fastened to our father's old belt around her waist. Her brown pants will need a wash, as will her white shirt.

I wet a bar towel and wipe dirt from her rosy cheek and neck. "Don't tell me Mika called in again."

"It's past twilight, and I haven't seen him, so..." She shrugs. "Guess he's not coming."

I tuck her golden hair behind her ear and wipe away the dirt over her earlobe. Mag takes after her mother, who might've been a fairy because no other creature in all the lands could be this beautiful, with a pixie nose, smooth skin, perfect round eyes with long eyelashes, and shiny hair that never seems to get damaged or dry, not even in the winter winds.

"Rock, paper, scissors?" I ask. I hate peeling potatoes.

"Sure," Mag says, and we play.

I lose and will have to peel the potatoes early tomorrow.

She winks one pretty green eye. "How did we do for the night?" Mag opens the drawer the holds our coins. A few silvers slide over the wood. Not as many as we need to keep the lights on since the southern rebel problem has cut into our business. Most travelers aren't on their way to Lyan for vacation or business. Instead, they're seeking refuge there, and since most of the south is plagued by the same rebellion that's been going on for over a turn now, the king increased the taxes for the rest of us midlanders and northerners. The tavern and the few rooms we offer upstairs that make up our inn aren't covering the extra cost.

I rub her shoulder. "The soldiers will return."

The drunk lifts his head, showing chapped lips in the shadows of his cloak. He snorts. "They did return."

I frown. "What do you mean?"

"I'm it."

Giggling nervously, I hold out my palm. "Pay up and go rest. Breakfast is served early."

He snorts again. "You and I will be breakfast, and the horde serves itself after dusk."

Mag rounds the bar and sits next to the man. She yanks back the hood of his cloak, and it falls open to reveal the tattered red uniform of a soldier. A lieutenant, judging by the stars on his pocket.

"What happened?" I ask, a tingle of fear making my heart beat faster.

The soldier downs the pale ale and wipes his mouth with a sleeve, rests one foot on the floor, and wobbles as he stands. "The question is what *will* happen."

"What will happen?" I lean over the bar, and my sister leans in too, practically touching him.

He kisses her forehead. "The horde will come. They will consume. They will leave."

I lean back. "What do you mean, consume?"

"They're predators."

My sister and I laugh. We've heard the myth a million

times, but our father, the king's historian has been searching for these creatures for over ten turns, well before anyone has ever mentioned them. He kept returning empty-handed and as punishment, a few turns back, the king chopped off his head.

Now, whenever anyone talks about devastated villages, devoured corpses, and ravenous creatures, they say it's the horde. But if our father found nothing, despite the threat to his life, they don't exist.

"There's no such thing as the horde or predators," I say.

"I saw them." He points to his bloodshot blue eye, and I note the crusted blood under his fingernails. "A creature with teeth the size of my fingers, claws, fur, bright red eyes, ripping through my buddy's guts...and eating."

"Gross," Mag says.

The soldier stumbles toward the stairs. "The horde is coming."

"If they're coming, why are you still here?" I ask. He's full of shit.

"Nowhere to run. The king will kill me anyway. I'd rather my family think I died in battle than have them watch my beheading in the square."

The soldier's footsteps echo in the now-silent bar. The last patrons, a family with a small boy, throw silvers on the table and rush out the double doors.

"Hey," Mag shouts as she runs after them. "Hey, come back! He's crazy. Don't listen to him."

"The horde is coming!" the boy yells, and with that, the refugees passing on the road before the inn scramble. Screaming and yelling ensues as people start trampling one another, surging toward the road that leads to the bridge.

Mag waves her arms. "Stop, stop! There is no horde. It's just people like us playing dress-up."

Grabbing the tray, I start clearing the table, knowing Mag

can't stop the madness. The word "horde" throws people into a frenzy. That's because they don't know the king like we do. Our father told us of the king's ruthlessness and that the king would protect his land, if not his people. He wouldn't allow the horde to pillage and seize his land, not after he conquered it with blood and magic.

Besides, the king commands medeisars, creatures of magic nobody can defeat. The predatory horde, even if they weren't a myth (and they are) are no match for those creatures or for the king, who is said to be able to kill thousands with a single sweep of his hand. Father has seen it, and so I believe it.

Despite the danger to his life, my father couldn't find the horde.

They don't exist.

"They're a myth," I say out loud into an empty tavern.

Mag returns, grabs a bottle of our cheapest whiskey, and sits at the bar. She pours a pair of shooters.

We down them, then slam the glasses on the bar top. Whiskey burns down my throat, and I chase it with water.

"Let's clean up," Mag says and starts unraveling her messy braid. "You wake up early and peel the potatoes, and I'll cook breakfast."

"For our one guest?"

She smiles. "And us."

I smile back. "And us."

She presses a warm, callused palm over my cheek and pecks my nose. "Me and you, sister," she says. "We keep going no matter what. Right?"

"Right."

"The horde is a myth," she says.

"The horde is a myth. The monsters are a myth," I repeat. No, really, they are.

. . .

… until they're not.

To be notified when this book releases, subscribe to my newsletter and I'll send you an email. While you wait for this story you are welcome to check out some of my other books. Here's a super short fast sexy snippet of Blind Beast Mate, my first book back from 2016 =D.

MEET THE ALPHA BEAST

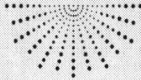

A SNIPPET FROM BLIND BEAST MATE

*J*amie

I'd almost kidnapped Rey straight out of her home, put her on my bike, and driven her to my house. That was how crazy I'd been when I first saw her smile. For us—the beasts from faraway planet Tineya— mating was a simple process. You saw a female, you felt she was your female, you took the female and made her yours. Making her yours meant conquering her pussy with might, fucking her to oblivion to get her into heat. That was our whole purpose as mated male beasts. To conquer our mate's pussy and get our mates pregnant with little beast babies.

We never told the communities we depended on their females for mating. We couldn't tell them we needed *the* girl and not any girl. We'd told them we took girls as pairs as if we could choose between many, even went as far as buying random women and putting them in the cities. It kept the power in our hands, or they'd try to fuck with us. Or hurt our mates.

Vice—the ass—had lost his mate before he'd even claimed her. We'd been looking for her all over this godforsaken land. We came to Rey's community in search of Vice's mate but found mine instead. I couldn't get Rey out of my mind, and the fact her uncle wouldn't let her talk to us, wouldn't let her join us for lunch, made me want to kidnap her even more.

I didn't ask him to pair her with me the same day. Instead, I'd listened to my brother Vice when he'd advised against mixing with scum the likes of her uncle. He'd said to be certain Rey was mine before asking for her. I went back home and couldn't get a wink of shut-eye all night. What if she ran off like Vice's mate had, and I couldn't find her? Naturally, this idea made me crazy.

Early the next day, I yanked one of their priests out of his bed so he could draw up the pairing papers. I rode back to her community with said papers and a case of money I'd strapped to my bike. Her uncle, the greedy bastard, had taken all of five minutes to sign the papers and take the money, but he held my mate for another week. Motherfucker.

But she was here now. Click!

MILANAVERSE

Connect with me by joining over ten thousand readers on my mailing list **HERE!**

Read the complete Tribes Series:

Marked #1, Stolen #2, Lured #3, Captured #4, Consumed #5, Arked #6

Read the complete Beast Mates Series:

#0 Virgin - FREEBIE, #1 Blind, #2 Wild,

#2.5 Goddess, FREE via my Mailing List,

#3 Sent, #3.5 Their, #4 Caught, #5 His, #6 Free.

Read the Complete Horde Series:

#1 Alpha Breeds, #2 Alpha Bonds, #3 Alpha Knots, #4 Alpha Collects

The Complete Hordesmen Series:

Hunger #1, Terror #2, Sidone #3, Fever #4, Dreikx #5, The Blind Hordesman #6

Read the complete Dragon Brotherhood:

Rise #1, Burn #2, Storm #3, Fight, #4

Short stories in IADB World: Jake 1.5, Eddy #2.5

Read the complete Age of Angels series:

Court of Command, #1 • Court of Sunder, #2 • Court of Virtue, #3

ABOUT THE AUTHOR

Milana Jacks grew up with tales of water fairies that seduced men, vampires that seduced women, and Babaroga who'd come to take her away if she didn't eat her bean soup. She writes sci-fi fantasy romance with dominant monsters from her home on Earth she shares with Mate and their three little beasts.

• She entertains the readers on her mailing list as they await for books in the series. If you want in, join other readers at http://www.milanajacks.com/newsletter/ •

Meet me at
www.milanajacks.com

Printed in Great Britain
by Amazon

15861302R00109